I0831174

AGP

BLACK | LIMINAL | GROUP | FRAMEWORKS

abbycat group

&

PUBLISHING

BRANDS

PALM DESERT | MARIN | HOLLYWOOD

STORIES BUILT TO **LAST**

abbycat group
&
PUBLISHING
BRANDS

SINCE 2025

Violent Crimes

AGP

JACK CHASE

abbycat BLACK

VIOLENT CRIMES

The Butcher of Westchester

THE FIRST **JAMES PRINCE** NOVEL

Published by Abbycat Black
An imprint of Abbycat Group LLC, operating as AGP | Abbycat Group & Publishing Brands
Palm Desert, California
www.abbycatgroup.com

ISBN 979-8-9986388-8-6 (Hardcover)
ISBN 979-8-9986388-2-4 (Paperback)
ISBN 979-8-9986388-3-1 (eBook)
Library of Congress Control Number: 2025909275

Cover design by FRAMEWORKS
Book design by FRAMEWORKS
Text set in EB Garamond & Bebas Neue

First edition, May 2025
First trade hardcover edition, November 2025

Printed in the United States of America

10 9 8 7 6 5 4 3 2 1

FOR MY TORTIE BABY, **MULAN**

"THERE ARE SOME CRIMES THAT ARE SIMPLY TOO **CRUEL**, TOO **SADISTIC**, TOO **HIDEOUS** TO BE FORGIVEN."

JOHN DOUGLAS

TABLE OF CONTENTS

FROM THE PUBLISHER

THIS NOVEL CONTAINS REALISTIC DEPICTIONS OF **BRUTAL VIOLENCE**, **SERIAL MURDER**, **DOMESTIC ABUSE**, **EXPLICIT REFERENCES TO CRIMINAL SEXUAL ASSAULT**, AND **SUSTAINED PSYCHOLOGICAL TRAUMA**.

READER DISCRETION IS **STRONGLY ADVISED**.

FOREWORD

To this day, I don't know *why* this particular story demanded so much from me, or why it nearly undid me. It certainly wasn't morbid obsession. I've always leaned toward darker subject matter, yes, but I've never been interested in glorifying violence or trafficking in pulp. Frankly, I'm repelled by true crime. Additionally, I don't write genre fiction. To me, genre is a vehicle; it serves me, not the other way around. What compels me is character. And in this case, they all but wrote themselves. Agent Prince, with his self-loathing isolation, his arrogant compulsion to test himself against evil, his guilt. Richard, with his volcanic rage, his gloom, his ruthless drive bordering on derangement.

To follow them down into their darkness was less a choice than it was inevitable.

The drafting was rigorous, infuriating, cathartic—punishing, frankly. A first-time novelist with more ambition than sense, I drove myself into dangerous sleep deprivation from late April of 2025 to the beginning of June. When I *could* sleep, I endured nightmares; unspeakable, allegorical, apostolic. In one, a fair-haired girl led me down an endless blood-red staircase in a deserted Manhattan cathedral, whispering with a blonde man about what to name the Antichrist—at least, until they realized I was there. My office turned arctic between the hours of two and four in the morning—the coldest room in my house to this day, even in the Coachella Valley. Objects vanished, particularly silverware. Music from another century drifted through the vents at the most godless hours of the night. It was as if the book itself wanted to prove the point: that evil rarely announces itself in grand gestures, but in quiet, disquieting intrusions.

Once upon a time, Americans gathered in the town square to watch hangings. Families brought their children. Vendors sold food. It was spectacle, no different than a ballgame. The appetite was always here; only the packaging changed. Today, suburban girls fall asleep to true-crime podcasts. Ted Bundy is treated like an anti-celebrity, as if that motherfucker deserves a star on Hollywood Boulevard. Depravity now just comes shrink-wrapped, streamed.

And that is the heart of *Violent Crimes.* Not violence packaged as entertainment. Not killers glorified. Not evil dressed up and made palatable. The people in this book aren't sexy. The things they *do* aren't sexy. They aren't icons, badasses, or brilliant masterminds of any ilk. Psychopaths, predators, murderers—these are but mistakes of evolution. If anyone comes away from this book thinking a killer is worth idolizing, they've missed the point entirely, and should grow up.

I sat with decades of FBI accounts, survivor testimonies,

family statements—four and a half decades of voices that don't leave you once you've heard them. I needed this book to be something different. Not another serial-killer drama, but something true. A story where repugnance and beauty, shame and dignity, reprehensibility and nobility could coexist in the same breath to form something cinematic, devastating, and excellent.

To do that, I had to enter the minds of predator, prey, and affected. Like an actor going too deep into a role, I couldn't just step out when the scene was done. But unlike an actor, there was no crew, no cast, no team to lean on, and I was doing it on a shoestring rideshare income. The effect this had on my relationships, my body, my mind was unprecedented. I'll tell you plainly: I cried through most of the chapters, sometimes while writing, sometimes after. Even now, I don't keep the book in my home for long. I sign copies, I send them out, and I let them go.

It will probably always be at the top of my favorite works of mine. But it is, without question, the darkest thing I've ever written, and may ever write. I told my mother I wouldn't do something like this again, not until later in life, if ever. Because this book doesn't just come from you. It *takes* from you.

Maybe, if one day I truly feel it in my heart and there's a reason beyond myself, or if the vision happens to land anywhere near the baseline this one set, I'll return to this territory. But this book, and type of book, may very well remain a standalone. And maybe that's what it was always meant to be.

It is one of my proudest creations. But it's *brutal*. And it breathes.

The truth is: demons exist. There are beings on this earth who walk among us, shop beside us, smile at us, who are simply not like you and me. There's no understanding it, and you shouldn't try to.

Ever.

So yes, evil is real. But it's also cowardly. It hides. It runs. It masks. Stripped down, it lacks identity.

My father once told me that even the smallest amount of black ink could ruin a white sweater. He was right. What he didn't say is that ink never lasts. It spreads, it stains, makes a big show.

But it fades.

Because what is darkness? Nothing more than the absence of light. It exists only when the light pulls back. But the light always returns.

Evil doesn't create. It can only feed. Which is why it cannot endure.

The sun always rises.

Always.

PART ONE

RICHARD

CHAPTER ONE

HOMECOMING

NOVEMBER 19, 2022

Richard Armstrong waited twenty feet from the moving walkway, hands buried in his jacket pockets. Westchester County Airport on the Saturday before Thanksgiving. Wall-to-wall bodies, recycled breath, the smell of burnt coffee and industrial cleaner.

He hated airports.

His left knee throbbed. Kandahar's parting gift, flaring whenever the barometric pressure dropped. Twenty-three minutes now, though it felt longer. Time moved like cold honey when you were waiting for someone you loved.

Six-two, broad through the chest. Gray eyes beneath a Jets cap. Beard streaked silver. The kind of build that came from years of carrying weight. In Bronxville they called him intense. His girls on the varsity team knew better.

The man who'd drive forty minutes for their away games. Who'd sit in hospital waiting rooms when their own fathers wouldn't.

The service weapon pressed against his ankle. Old habit. The doctors had a word for it. *Hypervigilance.* Richard called it common sense.

Then he saw her.

Evelyn emerged from the crowd like light cutting through smoke. Curls loose on her shoulders, wheelie bag trailing behind. Jean jacket over a black dress. Three months at Virginia had sharpened her somehow. Less girl, more woman. The way she moved through the terminal. Confident. Purposeful.

But the smile was the same. That crooked grin she'd inherited from her mother, along with the blue eyes. The stubborn set of her jaw when she was thinking.

Richard felt his chest tighten. His little girl who, somehow, was not so little anymore.

His mouth broke into a rare smile. The kind he saved for her alone.

She ditched the wheelie and ran into his arms with a squeal. He hoisted her up, hugging tight, kissing her cheek.

"Alright, alright," he said, setting her down. "Get your luggage, hon'."

"Ooh! Can we get pizza?" she pleaded, eyes lighting up at the nearby California Pizza Kitchen.

"Your mother's cooking dinner. She'd kill me."

"Meatloaf?" Evelyn rolled her eyes.

"C'mon." He turned toward the exit. "She's been waiting all day."

"Fine," Evelyn conceded with a fake pout. She grabbed her bag, returned to his side. Richard palmed the back of her head, kissed her hair.

"I don't know how you eat that crap anyway," he chuckled. She shoved him playfully.

Coasting along I-684 S in his 2014 Dodge Ram, Richard watched Evelyn in the passenger seat, cross-legged, face buried in her phone, for just a beat too long.

"You okay, Dad?" she asked, catching his stare.

He nodded. "Just glad you're home, baby girl."

She smiled. For a moment she was seven again, missing her front teeth, asking him to check under the bed for monsters. "Me too."

"Wanna tell me about school?"

"What about?"

"Friends?" He shrugged.

"Yes, Dad, I have friends."

"Any boys?"

She looked up.

"Uh-oh," he chuckled. "C'mon, spill it."

"Nothing to write home about."

"Good, 'cause if you did, I'd be shining my Remington instead of spending time with your mother."

"Jesus, Dad."

"I'm kidding."

"Are you?" Something serious entered her voice. "Because I'm not a little girl anymore. You know that, right?"

Richard's knuckles whitened on the steering wheel. "I know, honey."

"Really?" She tucked her phone away. "Because sometimes I feel like you still think I'm twelve."

Richard swallowed. "I just worry about you, Evie. World's a dangerous place."

"So you keep telling me." She sighed, staring out the window. Bare trees and gray sky rolled past.

They kept on toward Eastchester, passing a billboard with a young woman's photo. Blonde, freckled, braces, smiling. Bold black letters screamed from the sign:

MISSING 17-YEAR-OLD GIRL

MILEY MCDERMOTT

$10,000 REWARD

CALL (914) 337-0500

Evelyn preempted the glance. "Dad, seriously, I'm fine. You've got to stop seeing danger everywhere. It's starting to get weird."

The words stung. Every father's dilemma distilled: *how much truth could you share without breaking what you were trying to protect?* He'd seen enough evil to fill a dozen lifetimes. But Evelyn lived in a different world. One where missing girls were statistics, not prophecies.

"Just looking out for you, Evie," he said quietly. "That's all."

Guilt flickered across her face. She softened, brushing a strand of hair behind her ear.

"Hey."

He stayed quiet.

"I love you, okay? I'm sorry. Everything's going to be fine. And you're not the only one who worries, by the way."

"What's your mother telling you now?"

"Mom doesn't have to tell me anything. Are you taking

your medication?"

"Awh, Ev—"

"Dad."

Richard sighed. "Not as much as I should."

"Oh my—"

"Evelyn. Drop it."

"I wasn't gonna start!" Evelyn smiled. "Jeez, no wonder you're so grumpy." She started doing a mock monster voice. *"Me Richard. Me hate Thanksgiving. Rawr!"*

A laugh escaped from his chest, and before they knew it, they were both laughing uncontrollably.

"Honestly," Evelyn laughed, "let's start with listening to the doctor before worrying about serial killers and the end of the world."

Within town limits, Richard pulled into his usual gas station. An Exxon on New Rochelle. The truck shuddered to a stop at one of the outer pumps.

"Can you grab me some Twizzlers for later?" Evelyn asked.

"Yeah." Richard cracked the door, hopped out, tilted his Oakleys down.

He lumbered on to the market, feeling for his wallet. Evelyn stayed in the car, responding to Snapchats.

A silver Prius rolled into the lot. Parked opposite the Ram. Out stepped William Baker, son of car collector Morris Baker. William—who everyone still called Billy, whether he liked it or not—was a towering, thickset man who dressed a bit like a Baptist pastor, often donning a short-sleeved white button-up and corduroy pants with a set of Windsor glasses to really put the lid on it. He was a decently handsome guy in the twilight of his thirties, albeit a bit mousy, who kept his salty black hair combed slick and beard neat as all hell.

He also happened to be Evelyn's former eleventh-grade biology teacher.

Billy squinted. "Evelyn?"

She twisted her neck. "Mr. Baker?"

Billy laughed. "I thought that was you."

"I thought I saw you heading out of town earlier."

"Sorry?"

"The other direction. Like, twenty minutes ago."

Baker shrugged. "I've been at the school all day, Evie. Must have been someone else."

"Yeah. I guess."

"Here for the holiday?"

"Yep. Here for the gas?"

Billy shrugged. "Teachers need to get around too." He gave the Prius hood a smack.

"Honestly, I always figured you just slept there."

"Someone's got to use that dusty sofa in the coffee room."

She giggled, felt her cheeks turn red. *Christ, am I flirting?* Truth be told, she, like a good many of her peers, had had a bit of a schoolgirl crush on him. His class had always followed lunch, running energetic and light as they all cooled down in the dimmed, air-conditioned lab. As a teacher, he was extraordinarily bright and effective, with a dorky, boyish, and self-effacing side that, combined, left them swooning and fidgeting in their plaid skirts.

Of course, the bar hadn't been high. The rest of the staff were relics, stumbling around the copier like it was a bomb.

But there was something about him that made her feel *seen*. Like he recognized something in her that others missed.

"Billy?" she heard her father say.

Here we go.

Evelyn sank back into her seat and watched as the two men shook hands, exchanged some how-the-hell-are-yas, and did that thing men do when they turn dead serious on a dime, hitch their belts, and talk shop about God knows what. After a while, Billy began to head in for the clerk himself.

"Have a good one, y'all."

"Happy Thanksgiving, Mr. Baker!" Evelyn shouted.

"Happy Thanksgiving, Miss Virginia. And call me William."

He shot her a wink. She smiled.

Something in that wink—subtle, yet too familiar—made her stomach flutter with both excitement and unease. She pushed the feeling down as her father returned to the car.

"You know Baker well?" Richard asked, sliding into the driver's seat.

"He was my bio teacher. Everyone knows him."

"Seemed awfully friendly."

"He's nice to everyone. Don't go all SEAL Dad on me."

As they pulled away, Richard checked the rearview. Baker was still standing there. Watching.

That smile hadn't moved an inch.

CHAPTER TWO

PROMISES

Janet Armstrong fiercely chopped vegetables by the sink in their cozy two-story Dutch Colonial on Lookout off Park Avenue, tossing the occasional carrot slice to the indignant Zeus, a seven-year-old all-black German Shepherd. Janet was the kind of beautiful that didn't have to try. She kept fit, holding a tight, efficient frame, with blonde hair tied back in a ponytail, streaked just enough with silver to catch the light. Her face had warmth, though the kind built on structure: sharp, serious, carved with the lines of motherhood and the silent wear of marriage.

She met Richard sophomore year of college while playing DIVISION I volleyball for Princeton, where he studied journalism. He was brash and daring; extraordinarily funny; highly intellectual and introspective; and devastatingly handsome. Her mother adored him immediately, even yanking Janet aside in the kitchen after he first attended dinner at their Massachusetts home to whisper that she had better marry that man.

Beneath the brass lay an irresistible vulnerability; Richard was an only child of a particularly difficult single mother with a preoccupation for hard liquor, cigarettes, and nights out at the bowling alley, and in many ways, he had always sought a home—one he found with Janet and her affable parents. The two fell quickly and hard, graduating together and marrying just a month before he shipped off for the SEALs. A month later, she discovered she was pregnant with their Evelyn.

In many ways, she still considered Richard to be the love of her life. Nonetheless, years of active service along with its take-home behavioral residuals and sometimes up to half a year absent from her and Evelyn for the first thirteen years of their marriage had undoubtedly strained their relationship, and one left viciously untreated. Despite Richard's diagnosis of clinical depression with psychotic features at thirty-two by a Navy counselor, he vehemently, almost religiously, refused the idea of therapy, let alone fucking couples counseling. Couple that with low testosterone and deeply embedded trauma ranging from a narcissistic mother to the violent tours overseas, and you had a divorce attorney's wet dream. Nonetheless, neither party seemed to possess what was either the energy or communicative ability to even open that Pandora's box.

A knock at the door.

She wiped her hands on a dish towel and opened it to Martha Miles, smiling behind a foil-covered tray.

"Pumpkin bread," Martha said. "Figured you might want something sweet, with your daughter coming home and all."

"That's so thoughtful, Martha," Janet said, graciously accepting it. "Come in for a minute?"

Martha stepped inside, eyes drifting across the polished living room. "Place looks wonderful, honey. You've been busy."

"Trying to make everything perfect," Janet said. "First holiday with her home from college."

"The Baker twins were like that," Martha said, settling onto a barstool. "Left town, came back different. Morris could barely handle them."

Janet paused. "I thought Mr. Baker was an only child."

"Oh no. Morris had two boys. Identical. Of course, William made something of himself. The other one... well, some trouble, years back. Nobody talks about him anymore."

Janet filed the information away in that part of her mind where she stored the neighborhood's unspoken secrets: the affairs, the drinking problems, the children who'd disappointed their parents in ways that couldn't be forgiven. Martha went on about the neighborhood, the cold front coming in, and whether the post office was still losing mail. At seventy-eight, she moved on hips that belonged in the Smithsonian and caught whispers with ears sharp enough for Richard's spec-ops toolkit, a relic and a surveillance device bundled into one nosy old woman. The moment passed. Eventually, she made her way home.

At a quarter to four, the front door creaked open. Zeus exploded from the kitchen, barking hard, nails skidding across the floor as he charged the entryway.

Richard and Evelyn braced for the benevolent beast's affection as he zeroed in on his sister, hopping up on his hind legs and sinking his claws into her chest. She laughed the pain off, eyes twinkling with love for the canine she had leaned on since her eleventh birthday, when her father brought him home at just three months and nineteen pounds. She named him herself, having been obsessed with the Percy Jackson book series at the time.

"Hi, baby!" Evelyn squealed, fondling his massive head with her comparably brittle hands as he drooled all over her top. Richard smiled and pressed on into the house, setting his daughter's wheelie down by the living room sofa.

Evelyn pushed Zeus off and made a beeline for the kitchen with him trotting adoringly at her heels.

"Mom!"

"In here, honey!"

Evelyn rounded into the kitchen where her mother bolted to hug her tightly with closed eyes.

"Oh, baby," Janet gushed. "I missed you so."

"Me too," Evelyn said into her mother's neck. "I'm happy to be home."

"You hungry?" Janet asked, separating back over to her cutting board.

"Starving!" Evelyn said, hanging her backpack on an island stool.

"Go sit in the dining room," Janet said. "I'll bring you a plate. Your dad and I will join you in a second."

Evelyn did just that as Richard loomed in the kitchen, snuffing out Janet's euphoria like a candle. Twenty years of marriage had taught her to read the way his shoulders squared when the night had already been decided.

"What took?"

"Flight ran late," he replied, flat. "What do you want from me?"

"Oh, Jesus, will you stop?" she snapped. "I was just *asking*."

Richard loudly threw his keys onto the counter. "I'll be

in the dining room," he said gruffly, bowing out.

Janet leaned on the counter with her arms crossed. Rubbed her eyes. Let out a long breath. Then she went back to dinner.

The weight of their dysfunction settled on her shoulders, never something she grew used to; each time it struck fresh, as if surprise were part of the pain. She thought of the therapist's card still hidden in her wallet, of all the unsaid words piling between them. She glanced at the kitchen window, the one Richard always nagged her for leaving open. Tonight she'd leave it cracked, just to feel in control of something. Marriage was a series of small rebellions and even smaller surrenders—the window was hers, the loaded weapon under their bed was his. They'd carved up their fears and claimed them like territory.

The three sat at an oval mahogany table, its surface charmingly weathered. Crafted in 1935 Poland, it had been passed down by Janet's Holocaust-surviving grandmother as a housewarming present when the couple bought the place in 2005. Above it hung a Colonial-style chandelier, timeless in its elegance. A few feet away, the grandfather clock ticked faintly like a heart too proud to stop.

Richard silently sat at the head with a longneck Old Style, with Janet and Evelyn opposite each other on the sides, as they picked away at Janet's meatloaf, mac 'n cheese, and diced asparagus.

"Sarah invited me to a party tonight," Evelyn stated, scarfing up the mac 'n cheese like a refugee.

The two parents shared a look. Janet cleared her throat.

"At whose house?" she asked, taking the lead on this one.

"Dylan Smith's, I think," Evelyn replied, mouth full.

"Oh... Is Dylan, uh, in school?" she asked, playing dumb.

"I think he's taking a gap."

"Got it," Janet said, returning to her plate and biting her tongue. Dylan Smith had a less-than-esteemed reputation in Bronxville as its token upper-class burnout, with more THC and street-brand psychedelics running through his body than blood. At just eighteen, he'd burned through two $90,000 cars with his infantile record already boasting a DWI. His parents were both powerful, high-ranking businesspeople in their respective industries, and what they had most in common was that they were never home.

Janet thought little of the boy. She'd watched too many of Bronxville's golden children crash and burn, their parents' money cushioning the fall but never erasing the wreckage. Dylan was trajectory without destination: a cautionary tale dressed in designer clothes.

Richard, on the other hand, harbored a reasonable fondness and forgiving attitude toward the young man due to his God-given prowess on the basketball court as a point guard, leading his senior season with 18.3 points per game and dragging the Bronxville Tigers to the semi-finals. Sports were the universal language Richard still spoke fluently. On the court, everything made sense: rules, boundaries, winners, losers. It was messier in the real world, where talent couldn't always save you from yourself.

"You sure you don't want to just stay in and watch a movie?" Janet proposed. "It's gonna get below thirty tonight, hon'."

"Tomorrow night," Evelyn negotiated. "I promise."

"Sweetie?" Janet deferred to Richard.

He shrugged. "Just be home by eleven."

"I will," Evelyn promised.

Janet conceded. "Guess that settles it. Just be safe."

The tension in Richard's jaw betrayed his casual tone. Every instinct screamed at him to lock her in her room, to wrap her in bubble wrap and hide her from a world that devoured innocence like candy. But you couldn't raise a daughter in a bunker. You couldn't love someone into safety. All you could do was teach them to run fast and hope they never had to.

Later, when Evelyn bounded upstairs to change, Janet all but cornered Richard in the kitchen.

"You let her go awfully easy," she observed, arms crossed.

Richard sighed, retrieving another beer from the refrigerator. "She's eighteen, Janet."

"Since when have you cared about that?" Janet kept her voice low. "Usually you've got a black site running background checks on anyone who so much as smiles at her."

"She made it pretty clear in the car that she doesn't need my protection anymore." He twisted the cap off with more force than necessary. "Said I need to stop seeing danger everywhere."

Janet's expression softened. She placed a hand on his arm. "Richard..."

"She's growing up, Janet. I can't stop it." His voice cracked slightly. "Much as I might want to."

Upstairs, they heard Evelyn on the phone, her excited chatter filtering down. For a moment, they were united in their shared concern, their shared love for the young woman whose childhood seemed to be slipping away before their eyes. It was the closest they'd been in months; not touching, but occupying the same emotional space. Two people who'd forgotten how to be married but remembered perfectly how to be parents.

"Just be ready to pick her up if she calls," Janet said. "No matter what time."

Richard nodded, draining half his beer in one swallow.

"Always am."

CHAPTER THREE

THE PARTY

Sarah Willoughby pulled up to the Armstrongs curb in her tattered, tan-colored 2005 Toyota Corolla, idling as Evelyn, wrapped in a purple parka with a black beanie, descended the sloped front lawn with her arms crossed, her breath visible.

Evelyn and Sarah, skinny and green-eyed with straight blonde hair, had known each other since they were six, and, in many respects, were each other's closest friend. Their natures complemented one another's, with Sarah's extroversion balancing out Evelyn's gloom. It was the kind of friendship that survived because of its contradictions. Sarah's recklessness grounded Evelyn to the world, and Evelyn's steadiness kept Sarah from floating away entirely. They needed each other in ways neither fully understood.

Sarah was popular with boys and particularly older men,

never short on stories of sex and hotel parties from as early as her freshman year. Meanwhile, Evelyn was more likely to be found curled up with a book in the mystery aisle at the library (certainly not the romance section) or binge-watching a true crime doc on Netflix, cross-legged in the center of her bed with a bowl of popcorn and her black hair tied back. Sarah was Prom Queen.

Evelyn was valedictorian.

Sarah extended her right arm to crack the passenger door open, allowing Evelyn to slip in.

"Heeeyyy, bitch!" Sarah squealed. The two hugged tightly over the emergency brake.

"So," Sarah said, falling back into her seat with a mischievous, wily smirk, "you ready?"

"I have to be back by eleven," Evelyn said, dumping her purse at her feet and clicking her seatbelt on.

"Yeah, yeah, no worries," Sarah assured unconvincingly, pulling her mirror down to apply a last-minute dab of blush. "Frankie's gonna be there tonight, y'know."

"Oh, God," Evelyn groaned in despair. Frankie Lopez had been Evelyn's one and only boyfriend throughout high school—a relationship that, in many ways, had been a miracle in itself, almost a bad joke.

Frankie Lopez, only son of steel worker and widower Roger Lopez, was a lean, hard-drinking one-man-army of a character; the likes-to-fight kid and proverbial James Dean of Bronxville, never without a cigarette and never without something to say, with messy, greasy black hair that shrouded angry, daring eyes, and scarred hands which sported a gallery of ill-advised tattoos he'd received over several stints in juvenile facilities as a boy. Even the biggest, meanest kids in town had once feared the five-foot-seven chainsmoker.

His mother had died violently when he was just nine, crashing head-on into an open pickup truck full of scrap metal. A large sheet of steel had flown through the windshield, internally decapitating her. In sixth grade, a little shit on the playground made a crack about it, and Frankie responded by breaking his wrist, spewing blood all over the sand and triggering a scream of agony heard three towns over. Needless to say, mouths were zipped from then on out.

The accident had been front-page news in Bronxville for weeks. Evelyn remembered being ten years old, watching her mother turn the newspaper facedown at breakfast, the same way adults suddenly stopped talking when children entered rooms. Death wasn't supposed to touch their insulated world, but it had, brutally and without warning.

Nonetheless, he and Evelyn, albeit off-and-on, had shared a unique and, dare say it, beautiful bond. She was the only person he had ever not been shy or awkward around. With her, the guard didn't drop. It *disintegrated.* He was extremely protective of her, and she in return. While others saw a bad egg, she saw sweetness and pain. In a sense, they nurtured one another.

That is, until August, when Frankie was forced to face the idea, let alone the fact, of Evelyn traipsing off three hundred and sixty miles to Virginia while he stayed to work with his checked-out father. Despite being thoroughly unfair, it could be said that he internalized it as a betrayal. Put lightly, it had ended sourly.

Evelyn felt a knot form in her stomach at the mention of Frankie's name. Their last encounter had been ugly. Screaming in her driveway, him accusing her of thinking she was too good for Bronxville, for *him*. The hurt in his eyes when she'd walked away still haunted her. Some wounds you carry in your chest like shrapnel—too dangerous to remove, too painful to ignore. Frankie was hers. The boy who'd shown her his scars, literal and otherwise, who'd trusted her with his rage and his tenderness. She'd left him anyway.

But there was more to it than Sarah knew. More than *anyone* knew.

"Don't worry," Sarah said, uncapping her lipstick. "I have someone new for you."

"Please no."

"Girl, yes!" she countered, running the red lipstick over her bottom lip. "He's very tall, very hot, and *very* dumb. He'll be perfect for tonight."

"I'm not trying to make Frankie jealous."

"I didn't say you were!" Sarah defended glibly. "Now, let's jet before my engine freezes. And, make no mistake, you're taking shots with me tonight, college girl."

Sarah geared into drive and pulled off.

Half a block down from the Armstrongs had been sitting a running, black 1980 Chevrolet Caprice, idling uncannily with "How Soon is Now?" by The Smiths drumming off its radio.

It began to prowl forward.

Sarah dragged Evelyn by the hand into the Smith's French Normandy Tudor mansion on Masterson Road. Hip-hop thumped as they navigated through the bumbling clusters of Bronxville's finest schmoozing in the sweltering foyer.

The two rounded into the massive kitchen, its quartz island littered with solo cups, bottles of liquor, and snacks pulled from the surrounding white pantries. A joint was being passed around.

The wiry, rat-faced Dylan Smith, in an unbuttoned Mets jersey, commanded the area by the sink with a fifth of Absolut at his hip like a ghetto Gatsby. He was chatting up a pair of twins before locking onto Sarah like a dog would a squirrel.

"Sarah!" Dylan bellowed, tossing back a swig and pushing past the twins. "My girl! How are you?"

He and Sarah hugged.

"'Sup, Evie?"

"Hi."

"Yo, Robby! Dickwad!" Dylan shouted across the kitchen. "Grab some glasses for the ladies, will ya?" He looked back at the two with a smile. "You guys ready to get fucked up?"

Three consecutive shots of vodka had left Evelyn's one-hundred-and-thirty-pound frame dizzied. College had taught her many things, but drinking wasn't one of them. The alcohol sat heavy in her stomach, making everything feel slightly off-kilter. She thought of her father's words about danger, how it could come from anywhere, even from her own poor decisions—*particularly* from her own poor decisions.

It was 10:06 as she stood under the arched entrance to the buzzing, cathedral-ceilinged living room, clutching a red cup to her bosom more for display than consumption. Sarah, conversely, had drunk double her intake and wandered off with Dylan.

Evelyn regretted coming almost immediately. The music was too loud, the house too crowded with people she barely knew anymore. She found herself scanning the room for Frankie, both hoping to see him and dreading the encounter.

The alcohol was making her feel sick rather than relaxed. She hadn't been much of a drinker in high school, and college hadn't changed that. Three shots on an empty stomach was a mistake.

It was then that a tall (an easy six-five), handsome, athletically built young man in a turquoise polo shirt with cropped brown hair and the flighty gaze of privilege approached her, hands half-shoved into the pockets of his dark jeans.

"Evelyn, right?" he opened.

She looked at him. "Yeah."

"Tyler," he said, putting out a hand. Evelyn shook it, flashed a polite but unmistakably unenthused smile, and clutched her drink even closer.

"Yeah, I don't know if she, uh... Sarah's a friend of mine. I guess she wanted us to meet?"

It hung oddly in the air. He cleared his throat.

"She says great things about you, y'know. That you're, like, really into books and stuff."

The giant meant well. Evelyn chose to bite. "What school do you go to?"

"Massachusetts," he replied proudly. "Yeah, I play baseball there."

Another polite smile. She looked back out into the sea of inebriated Upstaters.

That's when the world stopped.

Across the way, stoically seated in a large recliner, was Frankie, staring directly at her.

Evelyn's heart shot into her throat in an instant. Her palms broke out into a sticky sweat. Every tendon in her body began to tighten. A foreign, unpleasant feeling began to arise from the depths of her stomach and into her chest—almost like dread.

She set the drink aside. "Excuse me," she said breathlessly, breaking away from Tyler and almost tripping on a $3,000 rug as she descended the main downstairs corridor.

She opened the door to what looked like a bathroom. Three boys and two girls were doing cocaine.

"Sorry," she gasped, shutting the door again.

It was then that a giggling Sarah emerged from a bedroom under Dylan's arm.

"Evvvieee!"

"Can we go?"

"Whaaat? But, like, it's *so* early—"

"Sarah." It came out firm. "*Please*. I want to leave."

Sarah's smile faded, instead morphing into an ugly scowl. "Fine," she said, stumbling off from Dylan. "Don't have to be a bitch about it."

This was Sarah's M.O. God forbid the party should end, and if it did, she'd make it damn clear to you how she felt about it. That, and she had consistently been a nasty drunk. In fact, it might've been the only thing she was *ever* consistent in. Evelyn had weathered this a thousand times, no longer taking it personally.

"Can you drive?" Evelyn moved on.

"Yeah." Sarah reached into her back pocket for her keys, fumbling them onto the ground. "You want to leave so fuckin' bad—*let's go*."

Sarah snatched up her keys and walked ahead of Evelyn, who followed wearily.

They walked out of the party and into the driveway.

Sarah almost tripped.

"Sarah, give me the keys," Evelyn finally said.

"It's fine," Sarah replied absently, pushing full throttle now to the Corolla, as if whoever made it to the automobile first was somehow more fit to commandeer it. "C'mon."

"Evelyn."

She turned around.

It was Frankie, smoking a cigarette by the ajar door. They looked at each other for a while.

"Don't get in that car."

There was a softness in his eyes. Evelyn felt her heart flutter, wanting desperately for the courage to heed his words, to stay with him—

"Evvveeelyyynnn!"

She felt her shoes scrape in the direction of the Corolla.

It was that moment, that ostensibly measly, throwaway split-second in time, of random decision-making, that would rock the small Upstate town of Bronxville, New York to its very core forever.

As she walked toward Sarah, Evelyn caught Frankie's expression. The hurt, the betrayal, the resigned acceptance. Her step faltered. For a moment, she almost turned back. This was how lives changed—not with grand gestures or dramatic declarations, but with small surrenders, tiny failures of courage that accumulated like interest.

But Sarah was already in the driver's seat, the engine running. And something in Evelyn couldn't face confronting Frankie. Not here, not now.

She climbed into the passenger seat, avoiding Frankie's gaze. As Sarah backed unsteadily out of the driveway, Evelyn caught a final glimpse of him in the side mirror, still standing there, watching her leave. Again.

The regret was immediate and overwhelming.

Behind them, the black Caprice that had been parked down the street pulled away from the curb.

CHAPTER FOUR

THE DARK

Evelyn sat in silence as Sarah, reeking especially now of liquor and marijuana in the heated confines of the sedan, roughly commanded the wheel. Each brake was a jolt to the system; every curve a seemingly endless toss of fate. Half of her wished a state trooper would flash his lights at any second now, haul the crazy bitch off, and safely transport her home. Maybe then she'd learn.

But deep down, Evelyn knew no one was coming to save them. This was Bronxville at midnight. Patrol cars didn't cruise these manicured streets where money bought silence and problems disappeared behind closed doors.

"Shit!"

Sarah slammed her foot on the brake at a dime, viciously lurching Evelyn forward and almost sending the Corolla into a wipe-out.

Three feet ahead of the hood stood a rail-thin coyote, organs thumping beneath its matted coat.

Sarah gave it a honk. "Move, motherfucker!"

The creature sauntered off. The coyote's eyes had reflected the headlights like coins at the bottom of a well. Wild things didn't belong in Bronxville, but lately they'd been appearing more often. Drawn by something, or driven by something else.

Evelyn unclicked her seatbelt, her face white with rage.

"That's it," Evelyn said, snatching up her purse and opening the door. "Good luck."

Sarah sobered. "Ev', it's, like, a mile back still—"

"I don't care." Evelyn was fully outside of the Corolla now, double-checking her belongings.

"Evelyn, it's freezing—"

Evelyn slammed the door, shouldered her purse, and began to press forward.

Sarah cruised forward at two MPH and rolled down the passenger window. "You're really gonna do this?"

Evelyn ignored her. Sarah scoffed.

"Y'know what? Have fun. Your parents better not bitch at me about this. Remember this was *your* choice. Fuckin' priss—"

Sarah rolled the window back up and roared off into the night.

The roads were starkly empty, the neighborhood absurdly unlit. Evelyn located and stopped at a lamppost to dig around her purse under the yellow hue, clawing her phone out from the bottom.

Dead. Between the flight, thirty-five-minute drive home, dinner, and Dylan's, plugging it in had skipped over her busy mind.

"Fuck," she breathed. She threw the brick back into her

bag and kept on.

The cold air bit through her parka, numbing her fingers and nose. Each breath formed a small cloud in front of her face. The neighborhood felt abandoned, the big houses looming dark and silent on either side of the street. Only the occasional window was lit, a reminder that most of Bronxville was already settling in for the night.

Her thoughts drifted to Frankie. The look on his face as she'd walked away. What would have happened if she'd stayed? They could have talked. *Really* talked. About everything. About the pregnancy. About what they were going to do.

Now she was alone in the freezing night, without a phone, her decision to abort still weighing heavy in her stomach along with three shots of vodka.

The black Chevrolet Caprice rounded onto the block and rolled to a stop about fifty yards off, "Don't Answer Me" by The Alan Parsons Project softly carrying down the dark street from its speakers. Evelyn noticed it now and took pause.

The windshield was tinted black. She stared back at the faceless Caprice, its headlights resembling the glowing, slitted eyes of a jaguar in the brush.

It was watching her. She felt it all the way down through her lower vertebrae. This was how prey felt in the moments before the strike. That primal recognition that something was fundamentally wrong, that the natural order had shifted and you were no longer the hunter but the hunted.

She started walking again. On cue, the Caprice growled back up, prowling slowly in her direction.

Keep cool. Keep fucking cool.

At the end of the block, to the right, lay a dog-walking trail through a forest clearing. If she remembered correctly from cutting through with Zeus and her mother as a child once, it would take her over a creek and then spit her out into the neighborhood opposite.

The Caprice picked up in a trice, throttling forward violently now. Evelyn reached the weathered sign—PLEASE PICK UP AFTER YOUR DOGS—and hastily hooked a right down and onto the trail, mind blank and heart pounding. She tripped on a root and tumbled down a steep, jagged slope for what felt like an eternity, landing poorly on her right arm with a wail.

Her wrist shot hot with pain. Bone had broken through. Tears began to stream down her face, creating lines in the dust, as she lay, sprawled, belly flat in the dirt. Her purse lay ahead, its items scattered helplessly about. Her phone screen had cracked against a rock, the fractured glass reflecting her terrified face in jagged fragments.

She heard the Caprice shudder to a stop by the entrance to the trail, its brights illuminating the clearing and shining through the trees. She heard a door slam shut and subsequently, leaves crunching under boots. She managed to prop herself up with her good arm. As she attempted to get vertical, her ankle started sending rapid-fire messages to her brain that it was fucked up, too. With her wrist turning numb and her ankle on fire, she glanced over her shoulder to see a brawny silhouette standing at the mouth of the trail.

Her breathing turned short and shallow. She wanted to scream but had no throat.

Fuck the trail.

She tore off her parka and cut right into the woods in a sort of limped gallop, clutching her wrist. A low, edged branch slashed her across the bicep, prompting a searing pain and sending hot spurts of blood down her sleeve.

Now the screams came. Bloodcurdling, strangled cries, like a stuck deer. She looked back again. The flashlight beam cut through the darkness like a surgical instrument, precise and unforgiving. Behind it, the man moved with the confidence of someone who had done this before, who knew exactly how this night would end. A man was descending in her direction with a flashlight now, blinding her bloodshot, terrified eyes. She used the base of a tree to propel herself forward, hearing brush crash behind her.

Sweat would begin to flood her eyes from her brow, skewing her vision. Her legs would mimic jelly under the duress of uneven terrain in conjunction with a rolled ankle. Her broken wrist would trigger burn-up. And her arm, gushing like a hose, would soon fall numb and limp at her side.

It had all happened so fast. Before Evelyn knew it, she had been swallowed by the dark.

The man's heavy breathing was close now, too close. The beam of his flashlight swept across the ground, catching glimpses of her blood on the fallen leaves.

"Evelyn," a voice called softly. "Don't be afraid. I'm here to help you."

The voice was familiar. Almost soothing in its calm assurance. A voice that inspired trust.

Her racing mind tried to place it as she pressed herself against the rough bark of an ancient oak, trying to control her gasping breaths. The pain in her wrist was excruciating, the blood from her arm soaking through her sleeve and dripping onto the forest floor.

The flashlight's beam swept closer.

"You're hurt. Let me help you, Evelyn. I know these woods. I can get you home."

She closed her eyes. A memory surfaced. Distant but

unmistakable. And her blood ran cold.

When she opened her eyes again, the beam was directly on her face, blinding her. Behind it stood a familiar silhouette.

"There you are," the voice said with satisfaction.

And in that moment, as recognition dawned, Evelyn Armstrong knew she would never see her home again. Some knowledge arrives like lightning: sudden, blinding, irrevocable.

As the familiar voice spoke her name again, Evelyn understood that everything she'd feared about the world, every danger her father had tried to warn her about, had been wearing a friendly face all along.

CHAPTER FIVE

GONE

NOVEMBER 20, 2022

Still in yesterday's clothes, Richard roused just ahead of sunrise, laid up on the frayed sofa which sat pushed up against his wall of service medals. On the carpet below was a glass with about an ounce of whiskey still residing in it, albeit half ice at this point and with a dead gnat floating in it.

He sat up with a pounding head and screaming back, mouth dry as dust. He swung his gigantic legs over and planted his feet onto the carpet with a loaded exhale. He'd been up late drinking a fifth of Tullamore Dew and revising his latest piece for *The Bronxville Journal*, a traditional two-page spotlight on the town's upcoming Thanksgiving Day parade, which was a gig as cut-and-dry and prosaic as the event itself. He'd regretfully accepted the job for pennies from Eddie Goldman, the paper's stumpy, booze-soaked editor-in-chief with less working capital to burn than hair, while out at the local tavern and four ales in.

Sure, Eddie, anything for the town.

Fuck it. Kept him busy.

A flicker of irritation crossed his mind as he remembered Evelyn hadn't bothered to say goodnight when she got in. Probably thought he was passed out. Probably was, for that matter.

He lumbered out to the kitchen and felt a cold, whistling draft pulling in from the window above the sink. Janet liked to let the chill in after cooking dinner and, despite Richard's constant reminding over the years, never shut it. It always annoyed him.

Richard slid it shut. He ambled over to the coffee maker, unhooked the pot, and stuck it in the sink to fill up. He then locked it back in, drew an extra-large canister of Folgers Black Silk from the above cabinet, and dumped two-and-a-half scoops into a fresh filter.

While that brewed, he trudged upstairs to check on Evelyn and fetch Zeus, who cozied up with Janet in bed at 9:00 P.M. every night like clockwork.

But first, Evelyn. Wait, she'd always loved a good morning assault from the big dork. He stopped at his and Janet's bedroom where, sure enough, Zeus was sniffing at the door, primed to burst like a penned bull. He let him out. Janet was still in slumber, snoring delicately. He paused in his routine to study her. Even with her hair stringy and matted over her crusted eyes, sweat glistening on her forehead, mouth dumbly hanging open and leaking drool, she was still the most beautiful woman he'd ever seen. He resented their rift, though he knew damn well his thickheaded ways had commanded a starting position in it. Maybe the holiday would ignite some repair, and they could send their girl off as one this time. Maybe.

Of course, he'd been telling himself 'maybe' for years now; maybe they'd find their way back to each other, maybe love would be enough, maybe the war would finally let him go. Hope was becoming a harder habit to maintain.

He began down the hall. He hadn't heard Evelyn come in but, between the whiskey, Guns 'N Roses, and writing, wouldn't be able to assume either way.

He opened the door to her bedroom. To his moderate surprise and Zeus' bafflement, she wasn't there. Her bed was still made from the morning prior when Janet had obsessively straightened and spruced up her room before he took off for White Plains.

She must've crashed with Sarah. She was a smart girl who worked her butt off in school, steered clear of most nonsense, and, in his mind, had earned a little laxity. In fact, he just hoped she'd had some goddamn fun.

And he liked the Willoughby's. Jim was a fine man and Maria an even finer matriarch. Sure, their daughter was a bit of a live wire, but that's where his came in for balance. Hell, it had always worked out in the past.

He'd call her in a bit.

Richard and Zeus descended the stairs. He unhooked the pot, still dripping, and quickly poured himself a cup. They went out into the back and Richard lit a Camel Red on the veranda as Zeus pissed. He wanted to quit, but what the hell.

The sun began to rise.

Surely Evelyn was fine.

A small voice in the back of his mind whispered otherwise; the same one that had kept him alive in war zones, that had alerted him to danger before it appeared. He pushed it away. This wasn't Baghdad. This was Bronxville. The worst crime in the past decade had been when someone's gardener stole their lawn mower. And it was an accident. But even in paradise, darkness found a way in. It always did. Haller had learned that much from his years in the city; evil didn't respect zip codes or property values. It went where it wanted, took what it pleased.

Still, as he watched the sunlight crawl across the perfectly manicured lawn, that familiar weight settled in his chest. The one that told him something wasn't right.

8:00 A.M. rolled around.

Still nothing from Evelyn.

SportsCenter's *Gameday Countdown* buzzed on the living room TV as Richard, showered and dressed, choked down his third cup of coffee.

He'd since shot his daughter a text. *Everything alright?* Certainly, everything was. However, he knew he'd need something concrete to impart to Janet once she inevitably rose.

Come on, Evie.

Richard's knee bounced ceaselessly as he checked his phone for the hundredth time. No response. No read receipt. Nothing. He tried to focus on the football commentary, on the score predictions, on anything but the growing knot in his stomach.

Maybe her phone died. Maybe she was still asleep. Maybe she was avoiding him after their tense conversation in the car. The possibilities multiplied, each more benign than the last, as he tried to stave off the darker thoughts creeping in.

Zeus laid his head on Richard's knee, sensing his unease.

Then, 9:00 A.M.

Evelyn's phone was shooting straight to voicemail.

Something began to stir in Richard's stomach after the sixth dead tone. The silence on the other end of the line felt malevolent, pregnant with possibility. Each unanswered ring hammered against his chest like a fist, building pressure that threatened to crack something vital inside him. He wasn't a pacer, but here he was doing laps like a loon around the kitchen, which was deathly quiet aside from the dull, torturous ticking of that goddamn grandfather clock Janet loved so much.

Enough was enough. He navigated to Jim Willoughby's contact card and dialed him. It rang for a few seconds too long before finally connecting.

"Hey, Dick," Jim answered sunnily.

"Hi, Jim. Good day so far?"

"Can't complain."

"Yeah. Quick question for ya. Evelyn there?"

"Sorry?"

"Evelyn. She didn't come home last night. Is she at yours?"

There was a hesitant pause. "Not that I'm aware of."

"I only ask because they were together, y'know. Some party. She picked her up around eight. Could you check?"

"One moment." Jim held the phone away and called for Sarah. There was some indistinct shouting back and forth. After a while, he returned. "She says she left early, Dick."

"Left early?" Richard repeated, feeling the lightness of fear creep up in his belly.

"I don't know," Jim said, beginning to mirror it. "You

try calling her?"

"Six times." Richard stopped pacing. He pulled out one of the stools at the island and sat on it. "I'm sure it's alright. Thanks anyhow. Sorry to trouble."

"Ain't no trouble," Jim assured. "Let me know when she pops up."

"Yeah," Richard mumbled. He hung up, feeling as if ten thousand pounds was pressing down on his spine. He tried Evelyn again for the seventh time. *Hey, this is Evelyn. I'm not at the phone right now. Leave a message at the—*

"Hon'?"

Richard's bloodless face shot to the entrance of the kitchen.

Janet, hair tied in its usual ponytail, stood by the counter in a pink robe and zebra slippers, eyes calculating her husband's arthritic body language. The man looked as if he was on the verge of a stroke.

"Everything alright? Where's Evelyn?"

He stared back at her solemnly. He could not speak. Her brow furrowed.

"Honey, what is it?" she pressed, the first notes of fear entering her voice.

"I don't know," he finally said, the words catching in his throat like broken glass. This was how worlds ended; not with explosions or fanfare, but with three simple words that unraveled everything you thought you knew about safety, about family, about the fundamental order of things. "She's not home. She's not at Sarah's. Her phone's going straight to voicemail."

Janet's hand flew to her mouth, her face draining of color. "But she said she'd be home by eleven."

"I know."

"Did you check—"

"I checked *everywhere*, Janet," Richard said, his voice rising. "I've called everyone."

The implications hung in the air between them, too terrible to voice. Janet reached for the counter to steady herself.

"Maybe she met someone," Janet offered weakly. "A boy. Maybe..."

"She would have called," Richard said firmly. "You know her. She would have called."

Janet nodded, tears welling in her eyes. They both knew. Evelyn wasn't the type to disappear, to worry them. She was responsible. Reliable. A planner.

"What do we do?" Janet whispered.

Richard was already reaching for his phone again. His fingers trembled slightly as he dialed.

"Sheriff's department," he said, voice steady despite the panic coursing through him. "I need to report a missing person."

Sheriff Joseph Haller's day was just starting.

He was a large son of a bitch, filled out at six-two and two-hundred-and-fifty pounds with a belly like a bowling ball. He lived in a modest ranch-style home a block or so up from Bronxville High with his wife Maple, a hairstylist, and a nine-year-old Cocker Spaniel appropriately named Wilson.

His morning routine was unvarying. Minus Sundays, and occasionally Fridays if willing in the schematics of any ongoings at the department, he would generally roll (literally) out of bed by seven, put a pot on, take Wilson out and light a Seneca, run a shower, pull on his black uniform, fill up the fancy Thermos Maple bought him for his sixtieth birthday, light another Seneca, and he was off.

He'd then arrive at the department (a four-minute drive), park in the front, sneer at the leaf blowers, and then take his throne to be briefed by the wet-eared Deputy Marcus Nichols. *What have we got?* Well, nothing, really. A kid might've shown up drunk at the high school, or maybe Mrs. Griffen's cat got out again, or maybe a pair of liquored-up local boys sparred at The Flailing Crab again ahead of close, or... or nothing.

Well, there *had* been that one girl, a 17-year-old named Miley McDermott, he believed, who'd vanished into thin air up in Scarsdale earlier in the month, but that, terrible as it was, had been just that. Scarsdale. Bronxville was Bronxville, in its insular, predictable, and beautifully boring glory; and Haller, not a young man, was more than content with that draw-up. He'd had his fix of chaos in his thirty-six years serving the New York City Police Department. He didn't miss the street stabbings, babies in microwaves, or sloppy Section 8 homicides, and certainly not the mountains of paperwork which followed them.

It was Sunday. Haller sat at his kitchen table in his pajamas with a bowl of Cheerios and a black coffee, mindlessly crunching away as he perused the morning's paper with his rimless readers resting at the tip of his booze-reddened nose. Wilson was sunbathing, belly up, by the sliding glass doors which led out to the backyard. It was shaping up to be a pretty day and he was debating putting a twenty on the Giants at one after taking Wilson out for a light stroll around the neighborhood.

That's when his phone rang. He stared at it with contempt for a few seconds before setting the paper down and picking it up.

"This is Haller."

"Hey, Sheriff, it's Deputy Nichols."

"I know, Marcus. What's going on?"

"Yeah, so, I know it's your day off and all—"

"What is it."

"This guy called in. Said his girl didn't come home last night and he's bent up pretty bad about it."

"Who?"

"Sorry, Sheriff?"

"Who's the call-in?"

"It's Richard Armstrong, sir."

This gave Haller pause. He knew Armstrong; not well, but by reputation. Former Navy SEAL. Hometown hero. Coached girls' basketball at the high school. Had a temper, according to some, but kept it under wraps. Most of the time.

"Dick Armstrongs girl is missing?"

"That's what he's saying, sir. What should I tell him? He's in *real* bad shape, Sheriff, I don't—"

"Relax. Is he at the station?"

"No, we're at his, sir. Monica and I."

Haller looked at Wilson. Sighed deeply. Then unclipped his readers.

"Give me fifteen."

In Haller's thirty-six years with the NYPD, he'd learned to distinguish between routine disappearances and something worse. Teenage girls went missing all the time; usually they turned up at a boyfriend's house, or crashed at a friend's without calling, or took off to the city for an adventure.

But something in Nichols' voice triggered old instincts. And he couldn't shake the thought of that McDermott girl from Scarsdale, still missing after nearly a month.

Sometimes coincidences weren't coincidences at all. Two girls. Two families. Two communities that thought money and gates could keep the wolves at bay. Haller had seen this pattern before, in the city. Predators were patient. They studied. They waited. And they always had a type.

As he pulled on his uniform, he tried to push away the dark thoughts gathering at the edges of his mind. But the image of that missing girl's billboard kept flashing before him.

Deputy Marcus Nichols met Haller out by the Armstrongs driveway with his hands planted on his hips.

Nichols, God bless him, was a tall, scrawny feller in his mid-twenties who looked a bit like a human Q-tip if one could imagine such a thing, with cropped, gelled-down black hair which resembled that of a ventriloquist dummy or a vampire; sickly, almost yellowy pale skin; sunken cheekbones; and a paperweight torso, whose deputy blues appeared unnatural and bizarre on his long-legged, disproportionate body. When he spoke, it was in a nervous and unintentionally dubious falsetto. Haller remembered first meeting him and thinking that God had just not smiled on this boy.

"Where is he?"

"In the house, sir."

Haller pushed past him and walked inside. Deputy Monica Vega, far too pretty to be confined into a squad car with Nichols, sat comforting Janet Armstrong, still in her robe and slippers, on their living room couch. Richard was pacing again, now with a drink in his hand and a bit of a mad look in his eye.

"Dick, I understand you're worried about your daughter," Haller said. "You mind putting that drink down so we can talk, friend?"

"It's that fucking Willoughby girl."

"Excuse me?"

"It ain't like her, Sheriff." Richard cocked back the last of the liquor. "It ain't like her."

"Let's sit down," Haller said carefully. "I need to know everything."

Haller suggested he and Richard step into the kitchen. He ordered Nichols to stay put and for Monica to keep with Janet. The two men walked into the kitchen and sat down. Haller instructed Richard to start from the beginning, and *no more goddamn drinking*.

Richard spoke for ten minutes, starting from the minute he picked Evelyn up and down to the songs they listened to on the way home. He told her how she'd come into the house, rifled down some of Janet's cooking, and before he could even breathe, announced that Sarah Willoughby had invited her to a party over on Masterson Road at that boy Dylan Smith's house, who was alright. She'd been picked up at eight with instructions to be back by eleven. What did he do? Well, he had that parade spotlight, of course. And then maybe he drank a bit after Janet went up. Okay, he *did* drink a bit. How much? Oh, just a few. Okay, maybe more. And then he passed out on that horrible sofa of his that was terrible on his back.

"And you heard nothing after that?" Haller asked. "No car in the driveway? No door?"

Richard shook his head, shame crossing his features. "I was out cold. Goddamn whiskey."

"When did you realize she wasn't home?"

"This morning. Her bed hadn't been slept in. Called Jim Willoughby. Sarah said she'd left early."

Haller made notes, his expression carefully neutral. "Any boyfriends? Anyone who might have picked her up?"

Richard hesitated. "There was a boy. Frankie Lopez. They dated in high school. Had a bad breakup when she left for college."

"Lopez," Haller repeated, writing the name down. "That Roger Lopez's boy? From the trailer park?"

"Yeah," Richard said, his voice hardening. "That's the one."

"Were they in contact recently?"

"I don't think so, but..." Richard trailed off, then met Haller's gaze directly. "Sheriff, my daughter didn't run off with anyone. Something's happened to her. I know it."

Haller studied the man before him; the decorated veteran, the committed father, now reduced to panic and fear. He'd seen this before too. Sometimes a parent's instinct was dead wrong. And sometimes it was the only reliable compass in a case.

"We'll check with Sarah Willoughby first," Haller said. "Get her account. Then we'll widen the search. See if anyone else from the party saw anything."

"I'm coming with you," Richard said, already standing.

"Dick—"

"I'm coming with you," he repeated, no room for negotiation in his voice.

Haller sighed. "You stay in the car. Let me do the talking. I mean it. And for God's sake, no more drinking today."

Haller drove with Richard to the Willoughby residence on Paradise Road, Nichols and Vega tailing behind.

Once they arrived, Jim Willoughby welcomed the four

into the living room. Maria, a well-aging woman with strawberry blonde hair tied up in a bun, offered coffee, which Haller accepted, and then handed to a catatonic Richard to drink.

Jim called for Sarah, who descended the stairs and, upon seeing the three police officers and, more scarily, a stale-faced Richard, went bloodless in the face. Her father told her it was alright, and she nervously went to take a seat on the couch between him and Maria across from the hard-eyed Haller and a supporting Vega. Nichols held back with Richard by the flat-screen TV above the fireplace.

Haller went through the night with Sarah. Okay, they'd gone to the party and been plied with vodka shots. That was to be expected. Then Sarah wandered off for an unmeasured period with a boy, leaving Evelyn out in the living room of the sprawling Tudor. Fine. Then Evelyn approached her and vocalized a desire to leave, and then... then she did what?

"We got in my car," Sarah said. Richard's eyebrow raised sharply.

That's not what she'd told her father; at least, not exactly. But he decided to bite his lip and let it play out. So did Haller.

"And we started driving back."

"When you say 'we,' who was behind the wheel?"

"I was, Officer."

"Continue."

"We were driving back," she went on, "and, all of a sudden, she just... freaked out, y'know, and wanted out of the car. I tried stopping her, telling her it was cold and all, that we still had a mile left, but..." She trailed off and hung her head.

Richard couldn't help himself anymore.

"That's not what you said this morning," he said briskly. "You said she 'left early,' not that she effectively leapt from your vehicle."

Jim wanted to intervene, but this was news to him, too.

"I mean, she—I don't—"

"What? You don't know what you meant?"

"Dick, ease up—"

"Shut the *fuck* up, Joe," Richard snarled, quickly gearing back to Sarah as Haller planted his face in his hands. "Evelyn wouldn't have gotten out with a mile remaining without a reason. Were you drunk, Sarah?"

"Goddammit, Dick!" Haller bawled. "What did I—"

"Let her answer."

"That's a pretty heavy accusation, Richard—"

"Oh, give me a fucking break, Jim!"

"Okay, I think it's time for you to—"

"He's right," Sarah blurted. The room went silent. "I was drunk. And she was scared. So she got out." She began to cry. "And I left her there. I'm so sorry. God, I'm so sorry."

Sarah's sobs filled the room, her shoulders shaking as the truth spilled out. Her mascara ran in black rivulets down her cheeks. Jim placed an arm around her, looking stunned.

"Where exactly did she get out?" Haller asked, keeping his voice level.

"Near the intersection of Pondfield and Midland," Sarah managed between sobs. "By that little wooden bridge. Where the walking trail starts."

Richard went rigid. *The walking trail.* The one that cut through the woods.

"Show me," he said, his voice barely controlled. "Right now."

Haller shot him a warning look, but Richard was already moving toward the door, his face set in stone.

She began to sob. Haller carefully glanced at Richard, who looked about ready to snap the girl's neck. Nonetheless, he kept his lips zipped as Sarah's cries overrode any oxygen still left in the room. Haller thought about arresting her for DUI, but what good would that do? Haller, Nichols, and Vega thanked the Willoughby's for their time and fled out with a fuming Richard in tow, who went code red as soon as they stepped onto the lawn, shouting at Haller that they needed to coordinate a search now. Haller calmly told him that they needed to wait at least twenty-four—

"That's unacceptable!" Richard barked, veins dangerously protruding from his temple like blue cables. "Find my goddamn daughter!"

"Dick, you need to calm down—"

"You should be arresting that little shit!"

"I won't say it again. Pull your goddamn shit together, or I'll be bringing you in. Got it?"

It felt cold leaving Haller's mouth, but... but what? He wasn't going to have Richard come to blows with him in the middle of the neighborhood with two younger officers present. That would only exacerbate things, and uglily at that. Richard seemed to absorb the sentiment telepathically and backed off.

"Just take me home. I need to be with my wife."

"Of course."

On the way back, both men were silent, listening to nothing but the rubber slap the asphalt. But their minds—oh, their minds—were each actively wandering to the dark corners of Hell itself.

In the silence, Richard's mind replayed Evelyn's childhood; her first steps, her first day of school, her graduation. The way she'd looked at him when he returned from his final deployment, like he was her hero.

He thought of the girl on the billboard, Miley McDermott, with her braces and freckles. Missing for a month already. He thought of the walking trail Sarah had mentioned, how it cut through the darkest part of the woods.

For the first time in years, Richard felt real fear. Not the hypervigilance from his PTSD, but primal, visceral terror for his child.

Haller's patrol car shuddered to a stop in front of the Armstrong residence. Richard went to open the—

"Promise me you're gonna be alright, Dick," Haller said. "That you're not gonna do nothing crazy."

Richard became frighteningly still. He then met Haller's eyes with a haunting, empty expression, like a man on his way to the firing squad.

Or the one set to do the bidding.

It was a look Haller would think back to for years to come.

"Find my daughter."

It came out just as flat as his gaze. He cracked the door open, slammed it absently, and began to hike up his lawn. Haller went to say something, but the words fled from his mouth, and just as quickly his mind. Perhaps it had been something along the lines of "She'll turn up, Dick," or "We will." Haller was many things, but a smoke-blower was one he refused to be.

As Richard disappeared inside, Haller stared at the house, a feeling of dread settling over him. His instincts, honed by decades on the force, were screaming at him. This wasn't just a girl who'd wandered off. This wasn't a runaway.

"All units," he said into his radio. "I want a preliminary sweep of the walking trail from Pondfield Road to Twin Lakes. Now. And tell the county we're going to need dogs."

Haller's perfect Sunday, and hopes for another anytime soon, had certainly come to a glum halt.

CHAPTER SIX

THE SEARCH

NOVEMBER 22, 2022

The search was commenced throughout Westchester County on the following Tuesday at 8:00 A.M. Parish members, schoolteachers, students, and townspeople alike from all over Eastchester joined the sheriff's department in the probe for Evelyn Armstrong's whereabouts.

A food truck was dispatched to the front lines, allowing volunteers to rifle down scrambled eggs and black coffee. A *NEWS10 ABC* van from Albany would also materialize with an evening segment on the fire, interviewing civilians and deputies willing to speak.

The media had descended like vultures, drawn by the scent of tragedy in an affluent community where ugly things weren't supposed to happen. Cameras captured the anguish of parents who'd never imagined their manicured paradise could harbor such darkness.

Divers were deployed into the Bronx River and Hutchinson River. Vested canines were sicced into Twin Lakes County Park, Nature Study Park, and their surrounding brushes. Two Bell 412EPs roared above the dense canopy of the woods like black angels, their rotors slicing through the brisk air rhythmically like metallic birds amidst a sea of green. The sound echoed off the hills like thunder, a percussion of urgency that seemed to pulse with the collective heartbeat of everyone on the ground. Inside the lead chopper, one of the pilots blasted "(I Can't Get No) Satisfaction," the Stones tearing through the cabin as if daring the forest below to hide anything at all.

"This search precedes a separate high-profile disappearance earlier in the month of Miley McDermott, a 17-year-old student-athlete of Scarsdale High, in which the greater Upstate area was vigorously combed to no avail," *NEWS10* would preface, adding that, "the pursuit was regrettably disbanded after a week of dragging the rivers, and the case turned cold."

Cold cases were what happened when evil outmaneuvered good, when predators proved smarter than their hunters. Haller knew the statistics. After seventy-two hours, missing person cases became body recovery missions. They were already past that threshold. Evelyn had now marked the second vanishing within thirty days, and after corresponding with a few other town departments, a fear began to brew in Sheriff Haller's nicotine-yellowed gut that he may, in fact, have a madman on his hands. Serial killers were methodical creatures, evolving with each victim. They learned from mistakes, refined their techniques, grew bolder. Two girls in a month suggested someone who was no longer experimenting. Someone who had found their rhythm.

Nonetheless, the search for Evelyn didn't take long, and on the second day at exactly 11:13 A.M., a volunteer in a blue, sweat-stained cap ended the search with just two syllables:

"Body!"

CHAPTER SEVEN

HALLOWEEN

OCTOBER 29, 2022

"What are you looking at?"

"You," Frankie said with a soft smile. He lay on her dorm bed watching as she turned in the mirror, dressed as Dorothy from *The Wizard of Oz*. It was Halloweekend at UVA, and he'd scraped together an advance on his thin paycheck to fly down the night before. He'd missed her terribly; she had missed him just the same.

Their last meeting, back on September 17th, had been a disaster—accusations slung in her parents' driveway, him calling her a sellout, her spitting back that he was holding her down. Words that had sunk deep and stayed raw for weeks. Yet here they were now, laughing in her shabby dorm room as if none of it, and no time at all, had passed.

He'd packed light, still in yesterday's clothes: a Deftones

shirt from a show they'd attended in June, grease-stained jeans, and white Nike sneakers with blue swooshes. *Never Be Apart* by TEEKS was drumming at a low volume off Evelyn's speaker.

"What exactly is it you like about me so much?" she said, twisting her leg.

Frankie leapt off the bed. He plucked a pretzel from the crumpled bag on Evelyn's nightstand and popped it into his mouth. "What makes you think I like you?"

Her smile faded. "Don't you?"

He walked up to her, chewing unsmilingly. He then let off a grin, bits of pretzel stuck in his teeth.

"Yeah, kid. C'mere."

He pulled her in and kissed her deeply. She unlocked her lips from his after a moment, throwing her head back and laughing.

"Ew! Your mouth's full!" she cackled.

"You don't like pretzel?" he joked, planting kisses on her neck and tickling her on the waist. She squirmed in his hold and began to howl ferally with laughter.

For this brief, shining moment, all was right between them. The fight before she'd left for college, his accusations that she thought she was too good for Bronxville, for *him*) seemed like ancient history. They were just Evelyn and Frankie again, the unlikely couple who had somehow found something real in each other.

Her hand rested on her stomach for a moment. Evelyn had missed her period on the eighth of October, which, from the age of fourteen, had been as sure, seamless, and consistent as the goddamn sunrise. She'd convinced herself it was just stress from starting college. But the morning sickness that had started a week ago was becoming harder to explain. She needed to warn him, but not *now*. Not when things were finally good again. Some truths were grenades with their pins already pulled. Once she spoke the words, everything would explode. This perfect moment, their tentative peace, maybe even the last of whatever they still had together.

Her roommate, Madison Chandler, walked in with her keys jangling. Madison was an art student, with short, curly brown hair and gray eyes reminiscent of a husky, who wore black lipstick and a septum piercing, along with a stud on her tongue. She was the girl all guys secretly wanted to fuck the lights out of, but only noncommittally. As an experience; perhaps behind a theater curtain, or in a maintenance closet during a lecture.

And some did. She didn't mind. She knew the deal. She was as Bohemian as they come, a latent bisexual, and a bit of an adrenaline junkie at that. Bold, kinetic, and foxy as all hell.

"Interrupting something?"

They responded at the same time, Evelyn saying no and Frankie saying yes. Madison snorted and set her stuff down.

"You two are disgusting."

"Go scare some neighborhood kids, Madison," Frankie shot back. She flipped him off. He stuck out his tongue.

"Did you get my text?" Evelyn asked her.

"Yep." Madison reached into her purse and pulled out a tube of gold face paint. She turned her body toward Frankie. "Whisker time, Mr. Lion."

"No way," Frankie said.

"Price of room and board," she said with a shrug.

Frankie scoffed and looked to Evelyn, who (what did he expect?) vehemently nodded in favor. Frankie slumped his shoulders. Surely this kid, tough and scrappy as he was, wasn't going to let—

But of course, he did. The two girls paraded Tough Guy over to the mirror and, Madison wielding the brush and Evelyn a makeshift palette in the form of a Dixie plate, gleefully painted gold whiskers on his cheeks. They purposely gushed over him as if he were a little boy to make him blush, which worked. Madison facetiously pushed her luck with a mascara set, which Frankie flatly denied while holding back an admittedly charmed smile.

They left the dorms around 7:00 P.M. for a Halloween party up the street at Delta Gamma. Madison hadn't rushed, nor did Evelyn, but she had supplied the glorified bulimics with rave drugs by the pound all semester long (she was fucking a Charlottesville promotor), granting her a sort of unspoken membership. *Thank you, J-Dogg.*

The campus was thumping. Music drifted indistinctly from opened windows, mingling with ubiquitous laughter and chatter. The sky had transitioned from its warm orange hue to a deep, velvety blue as the sun began to set, and a scent of woodsmoke was wafting through the brisk Virginia air.

They arrived to the party at 7:15 P.M. Madison scurried off, in form, with a couple blondes to get blasted. Evelyn and Frankie, tied at the hip, floated out to the backyard, which was gloriously canopied with Christmas lights and flimsy Halloween decorations. Some frat guys played beer pong in the back. Two vixens in Cupid costumes offered cups of "jungle juice" to Evelyn and Frankie by a folding table, and they were off.

It was an idyllic evening. Frankie ended up bonding with a few Sigma Epsilon guys, drinking and comparing tattoos with one another. Evelyn danced with some of the Delta Gamma girls, her blue eyes twinkling under the lights. At a quarter to nine, Evelyn and Frankie said their goodbyes, and Madison, rolling off ecstasy, spotted them both wet kisses on the cheek as they fled out, throwing in a "Get it, bitch!" to a jubilant Evelyn.

Buzzed and content, the two walked together through campus, swaying back and forth from one another like yo-yo's. At one point, they were caught in the geyser of a broken sprinkler and became soaked. They found this incredibly amusing.

They finally made it back to the dorm, which was bathed in moonlight. They stripped their damp clothes and hung them on the windowsill. A distant aroma of marijuana was wafting through. Their bare bodies met magnetically, and they kissed with palpable passion and affection before finally collapsing into bed with one another and making love in the dark.

Afterward, Evelyn lay with her head on Frankie's chest, listening to his heartbeat as he drifted toward sleep. The moment felt perfect. Suspended in time, outside the complications waiting for them in the real world. Tomorrow he would fly back to Bronxville. Tomorrow she would return to classes and exams and the growing realization that her body might be harboring a secret that would change everything.

But tonight, for just a few more hours, they could pretend that nothing had changed. That they were still just Evelyn and Frankie, figuring it out together.

As his breathing deepened into sleep, Evelyn placed her hand gently on her stomach, tears welling in her eyes. She didn't know what to do. What would happen if her fears proved true.

It was November 12th, 2022, when they did.

She'd woken up that Saturday morning with blood

thudding in her temples and plodded down to the nearby pharmacy to purchase an early-result pregnancy test, dodging eye contact with the middle-aged woman that rang her up, and—

There she sat now, legs crossed on the communal toilet, with this fucking stick in her hand that was telling her something she didn't quite understand. Rather, something she naturally lacked the faculties to grasp with anything besides cognitive static.

It was positive.

This wasn't happening.

Except it was.

She stared grimly at the hideously blue cross cratered in the stupid plastic wand. After a while, she stuffed it in her purse, pulled her sweatpants up, and went back to her room, where she would sit on the edge of her bed and do some staring at the wall, and then, without really thinking, snatch up her phone to dial Frankie.

Her hands trembled as she scrolled to his name, rehearsing the words in her mind. How do you tell someone you're pregnant over the phone? She'd thought about waiting until Thanksgiving break, telling him in person. But that was two weeks away, which would put her at eleven.

Fuck.

Madison had offered to go with her to the clinic, but Evelyn couldn't bring herself to make the appointment without at least telling Frankie first.

He deserved to know, even if the decision was ultimately hers.

Across state lines, Frankie Lopez was just arriving back to Hudson Valley Trailer Park following a six-hour shift at McPherson's Steel Works in Tuckahoe (Saturdays were half-days). It was a quarter after noon when his 2002 Ford Taurus shuddered—painfully— to a stop in the muddy driveway. A neighbor, an old codger smoking a Parliament in a lawn chair, greeted him as he stepped out.

The Lopez residence was your standard manufactured home, with a weather-worn exterior and a roof that sagged a bit, and an attached porch which boasted a rocking chair, ashtray, and a windchime. Frankie trudged wearily up the hollow front steps, hanging on for dear life under his steel toe boots, and unlocked the door, which squeaked a bit as he pushed it open.

He stepped inside and dropped his backpack onto the frayed, cigarette-burned sofa, its beer-rusted springs groaning in protest. The interior could best be described as tired, more or less bordering on forlorn, with scuffed linoleum flooring, ingrained windows, and pitiful wallpaper from the nineties. It was a familiar scene for Frankie, yet he couldn't help but feel a dull pang of disappointment in his belly each time he returned to it.

The stark contrast between his life and Evelyn's had been a constant source of tension between them. Her family's Dutch Colonial, with its manicured lawn and polished furniture, versus his father's trailer with its cigarette burns and peeling wallpaper. Every time she'd visited, he'd felt a mixture of pride and shame. Pride that she would enter his world at all, shame that this was all he had to offer her. He'd memorized every detail of her house during his visits. The gleaming hardwood floors, the family photos in silver frames, the way her mother offered him dinner with a smile that never quite reached her eyes. It was a museum of everything he'd never have.

He flicked a light on, unclipped his cotton overalls, and turned for the kitchen, his footsteps reverberating off the thin walls. He reached into a cupboard for a mostly clean glass, filled it up in the sink with New York's finest, and chugged it. Just another day for good ol' Frankie, it was.

His phone began to ring in the back pocket of his overalls. He set the glass down, dug it out, and picked up.

"This is Frankie."

"It's me," Evelyn spoke in a muted tone, cross-legged on her bed.

"Hey, babe." Frankie began to putter. "What's going on?"

"What are you doing?"

"Oh, not much." He drew a cigarette from a pack lying on the caked-up counter and lit it. "Just finished up with work."

"Do you have a second?"

"Of course. What's up?"

"I don't really know how to... Remember the Saturday before I left for college?"

He took a drag, a muscle flexing in his cheek. "What about?"

She shut her eyes. A tear escaped and ran down her cheek.

Here it came.

"Frankie, I'm pregnant," she said brokenly.

The cigarette froze halfway to his lips. Time seemed to stop as her words hung in the air between them, three hundred and sixty miles apart yet suddenly connected by this life-altering revelation. The distance had never felt so vast. He could picture her sitting on that dorm room bed, probably crying, needing him to say something perfect. But perfection had never been his specialty.

"Well, uh..." Frankie cleared his throat. "That's, uh... that's good, right?"

She frowned. "Good?"

"... No?"

"Frankie, how the fuck is that good?" It came out nastily.

"I don't know what you want me to say, Evelyn," Frankie said, matching her tone and dousing the last quarter of the cigarette in the sink. "I thought you were on birth control or some shit."

"I was," she choked. "I was tired that morning after picking you up from the airport and I just... I fucking forgot, okay?"

"Oh, so now it's my fault?"

"No, I—" She buried her face in her free hand. "That's not what I'm saying—"

"Then what are you saying?"

"Look, I thought you would've wanted to know, I didn't—"

"I would've. And now I do." They both took a pause. "So, what's next?"

"What do you mean?"

"Well, you're gonna have it, right?"

"... Frankie, I can't have it."

"Why not?"

"Because..." She sighed, choosing her next words carefully. "Because we're too young, Frankie."

"So, what's that gonna look like?"

"I don't know yet."

It dawned on him. "You're gonna kill our baby."

"It wouldn't be a baby, Frankie, it's—"

"What is it then?"

"Jesus Christ, it's a bunch of fucking cells!"

"Just say you don't want it, Evelyn."

"It's not about wanting it, Frankie. I'm not like—"

She stopped herself.

"Not like what, Evelyn?"

"I don't know what I was going to say."

"Not like a white-trash, uneducated burnout who lives in a trailer park like me, right?"

"Oh, fuck you!"

"What, with your perfect little life and insufferable Ivy League parents?" Frankie snarled, voice dripping with venom. "You know, when you took the stage for valedictorian, if that stick had been any further up your ass, you would've needed surgery."

"Go fuck yourself, Frankie."

"What's the big plan, Ev'? String me along until you pluck out some safe business major, get your big white house, and pop out a few clones until you either drink yourself to death or he starts fucking his secretary?"

"Fuck. You."

"You know what I think you are, Evelyn? I think you're a faker. And you know what else I think? I think, deep down, you're fucking terrified that maybe, just maybe, in the shit with me is where you really belong."

His words cut deep because part of her feared they might be true. That beneath her achievements and ambitions was the scared little girl who'd fallen for the town bad boy because he saw through her facade. Because with him, she didn't have to be perfect.

Her voice became frighteningly calm. "You're right, Frankie. I do think you're a white-trash, uneducated burnout. And I can safely say now that the thought of having anything to do with you does terrify me. I'm hanging up."

"Say you don't want it!"

"Fine! Here it is: I don't fucking want it, you loser, delusional fuck!"

"You're a fucking bitch, you know that?" The words tasted like poison the moment they left his mouth. This was what his father had taught him. When cornered, when scared, when the world felt too big and your place in it too small, you lashed out. You hurt the thing you loved most because it was the only power you had left.

"What did you just fucking call me?!"

Frankie hung up and chucked his phone. Something shattered. He then proceeded to punch a bowling-ball-sized hole in the drywall.

Evelyn screamed into her shirt. Then she cried.

And cried.

Madison found her hours later, curled up, eyes swollen and vacant.

"He didn't take it well," Evelyn whispered as Madison gathered her into her arms.

"Men rarely do," Madison said softly. "But this isn't about him. It's about you."

Evelyn nodded, wiping her tears. "I need to make an appointment. Before I go home for Thanksgiving."

"I'll go with you," Madison promised. "Whatever you need."

Across the state line in Bronxville, Frankie sat on the porch of the trailer, chain-smoking and staring into the night. His father had come home to find the hole in the wall but hadn't asked questions. Roger Lopez knew his son well enough to recognize when not to.

"Whatever it is, son," Roger had said, handing Frankie a beer, "it'll look different in the morning."

But Frankie knew better. Some things, once broken, couldn't be fixed. Some words, once spoken, couldn't be taken back. He'd inherited his father's temper, his mother's stubbornness, and his own particular brand of self-destruction. The Lopez family curse: destroying everything good before it could abandon you first.

By dawn, he'd made a decision. If Evelyn was going to the clinic, he needed to see her first. Look her in the eye. Make one last desperate attempt to change her mind.

He would find her at that party over Thanksgiving break. He would make her listen. He would make her understand that despite everything—despite his anger, despite her fear—there was still something worth saving.

The baby. Them. A future he could almost see if he closed his eyes tight enough. It was worth one more try.

But deep down, in the part of himself he tried to ignore, Frankie knew it was already over. Had been over the moment she'd chosen college over him, chosen her future over their past.

Still, some delusions were too necessary to abandon, some hopes too painful to kill.

CHAPTER EIGHT

FOUND

NOVEMBER 22, 2022

The once-ordinary surroundings of Twin Lakes County Park now seemed surreal, bathed in a pale light which cast long, mystical shadows across the clearing. Yellow tape fluttered in the light morning breeze, marking off the barrier between reality and the insidious unknown.

Amidst the ancient maples and tangled undergrowth lay Evelyn. Discovered about five miles up the river by Jeff Ginsberg, a cashier at Ace Hardware. Naked by the stream. Her legs were lacerated and checkered with abrasions, and her wrist looked broken. There was also a filthy gash about four inches wide on her right bicep, jagged and crude. Dried blood was coated on the inside of her thighs, and her throat had been slit.

And her eyes. *God*, her eyes. They were flat, milkily transfixed, and heartbreakingly confused. Death had stolen more than her life. It had frozen her final moment of terror, preserving it like an insect in amber. Those eyes would haunt every person who saw them, a reminder that monsters weren't myths but neighbors. Her face had been beaten to a pulp and her hair, wet from the creek, lay damp and matted over her discolored forehead. Flies sluggishly traversed indiscriminately from her eyes, glass-like and frozen in eternity, to her forearms and down to her still fingers, curled in rigor.

The Bell 412EPs returned to base solemnly. Haller and Vega oversaw the developing scene as Nichols rallied his party from another trail back to the front lines.

Haller stood by the creek like a monolith as forensics began to set up. He'd met Evelyn when she was just thirteen with her father at the County Fair. She had been delightfully precocious; whip-smart, self-assured, and heedful beyond her years, yanking facile straight A's and already musing on college. He remembered jokingly asking her father if he was sure she was his, and walking away thinking that Dick had a good one on his hands alright.

He began to think about life.

How the hell was Dick supposed to take this?

The wind changed direction, carrying the scent of decay more strongly. Haller covered his nose with a handkerchief, watching as the forensics team carefully photographed the scene, documenting every detail of Evelyn's final moments. The forensic lead crouched beside her body, making preliminary observations.

"Throat was cut with a serrated blade," he said, pointing to the jagged edges of the wound. "Death would have been relatively quick. The rest..." He gestured to the other wounds. "Premortem, most likely."

"Time of death?" Haller asked.

"Based on lividity and temperature, between 1:00 and 3:00 A.M. Monday morning. But I'll know more after the autopsy."

Haller nodded, making mental calculations. If Evelyn had left Sarah's car around 10:30 on Saturday night, that meant she'd been alive for over twenty-four hours after her disappearance. Twenty-four hours when they might have found her, when they might have saved her life.

Twenty-four hours he'd wasted following protocol. Protocol was for paperwork and politicians, not for daughters dying alone in the dark. Every minute spent on procedure was a minute stolen from salvation, and now those lost hours stretched between him and sleep like an unbridgeable chasm.

Haller had meant to tell Richard and Janet himself. He'd even started the drive, cap in hand, rehearsing the words. But halfway to the Armstrong place, Vega called him back. More protocol. The body needed to be processed. Tagged. Bagged. He turned the car around.

Now the big son of a bitch was here anyway.

"Sheriff?" Vega said, approaching fast. "Armstrongs here."

"Jesus Christ," Haller muttered. "How did he—"

"Scanner in his truck. He heard the call."

Haller turned. Richard Armstrong was coming up the hill, red-faced and barrel-chested, eyes wide with rage and disbelief.

"HALLER!" he bellowed.

"Keep him back," Haller snapped. "For God's sake, don't let him see her like this. I mean it!"

Vega keyed her radio. Two younger deputies moved in, bracing for impact. Richard didn't hesitate. He swung on the first one, catching him clean in the jaw. The second tackled him, and it took all three of them to bring him to the ground. A pair of cuffs clicked shut.

"That's my fucking daughter!" Richard bawled, face buried in the dirt. "Let me see her, you sons of bitches!"

Haller didn't flinch. He couldn't. He turned toward the body bag. Zipped now, inert. Just a shape where a life used to be.

He reached into his coat, pulled out the old steel flask, and took a long drink. It hit like guilt.

Twenty minutes later, the inside of the squad car was silent. Richard sat cuffed in the back, slumped and hollow-eyed, sweat dried to salt on his brow.

Haller drove.

Neither man spoke.

It was the same car. The same road. But this time, there was no fight in Richard. No pride. Just a father, wrecked.

When they pulled into the driveway, Haller parked but didn't get out. He looked at Richard in the mirror.

"I'm sorry," he said quietly.

Richard didn't respond.

Haller got out and opened the rear door. Richard stepped out like a man twice his age. His wrists were released. No one said a word.

He walked up the steps and opened the front door himself.

Janet met him in the foyer.

For a long second, she just stared at him. Studied the way his face had folded, the tremor in his jaw, the void in his eyes. And she knew.

He tried to reach for her. Tried to say it.

But he didn't have to.

Janet's scream tore through the house, primal and

jagged, as if something had reached inside, and started ripping her apart from the spine. She pounded her fists against Richard's chest, sobbing, shrieking, howling, until her palm cracked across his face.

He didn't stop her. He just held on.

They crumpled together in the doorway, two broken people clinging to what was left.

And from the squad car, Haller watched, shoulders slumped, eyes rimmed red, the flask still warm in his coat pocket.

Mere hours later, Richard stood in the bowels of the Bronxville County Morgue, arms limp at his sides, as M .E. Kenneth Lieberman, an overweight, beady-eyed gentleman with jowls like a bulldog, began the process of unlocking her vault. The room was awful; cold, sterile, and frighteningly arid. A bite of purgatory, illuminated by blinding overhead lights and lined with metal cabinets. Richard wondered how many fathers before him had impotently loitered where he now did.

The morgue smelled of chemicals and something else. Something colder, more final. Richard's military training had exposed him to death before, but nothing had prepared him for this moment. Nothing could prepare a father for identifying the body of his child.

There was a loud clack, snapping him back to the present.

Lieberman carefully glanced at Richard.

"Ready, Dick?"

"Just do it, Ken."

Lieberman nodded and rolled the slab out.

Richard slowly approached the table, brow furrowing and eyes softening as he looked upon his daughter. The tarp had been mercifully enveloped up to her chin, and her eyes had been shut. He tentatively lifted the sheet (against Lieberman's advice) and bore witness to her cut throat. He winced and closed his eyes in horror, allowing a tear to propel down his cheek.

"I'll give you a moment," Lieberman said gently, and waddled out.

As soon as the door slammed shut behind Lieberman, Richard began to weep. He placed a trembling hand over her forehead, which mimicked an ice pack.

"Oh, baby, what did they do to you?" he cried, running his fingers through her knotted hair. "Oh, honey..."

That night, the image of Evelyn being carted out from the woods of Twin Lakes County Park would air on *NEWS10 ABC Albany*. The anchor's solemn voice described the discovery of a young woman's body, the ongoing investigation, a community in shock. They showed footage of the search parties, of the medical examiner's van leaving the scene, of yellow police tape fluttering in the wind. Miley McDermott's billboard also made the cut, once again raising the question on everybody's minds.

It spread like wildfire.

Doors were locked that had remained unlocked for decades. Children were called inside before sunset. Women traveled in pairs, clutching pepper spray.

And in living rooms across the country, parents held their daughters closer, grateful they were safe, guilty for feeling that gratitude in the face of another family's unimaginable loss.

On the Wednesday morning of November 23rd, 2022, the

autopsy of Evelyn Armstrong was completed.

The overpowering scent of ammonia tickled Haller's nose as Kenneth Lieberman led him down the basement corridor of Bronxville County Morgue. Their height differences were comical.

"How's Maple, Joe?"

"Good," he replied briefly. Haller already wanted this to be over. Places like these gave him the willies, and any man who would do it for a living even more so. "Where are we?"

"Right here." Lieberman stopped at STE 10 and wiggled a key into the big metal door. *God*, Haller thought. It was like being shown to your room in Hell. He wondered when he'd begin to hear the drowned, oscillating cries of the damned. Part of him believed he already was. *Wait, was that a...*

Haller shook it off and followed the fat man into the examination suite. Lieberman, right at home, sauntered over to the table in which Evelyn lay, freshly sewn back up the middle. Haller soured at the sight.

There was this young, beautiful girl, once brimming with promise and character. And this was her fate? To be ravaged, robbed of life, and condemned to a metal slab in this shithole? To drift and wane into history as but a cautionary tale? And a tale of *what* exactly? The kid did everything right. It made him sad. Angry. Furious, frankly.

He thought back to the crime scene. The savage, animalistic nature of it. What kind of man would, could, perform such atrocities? Could it even be said that this was the work of one? Or something else entirely? Haller was no stranger to the cruelty, hatefulness, or malevolence that strutted this mortal Earth. Vapidly or otherwise. But this...

This was evil. True, repugnant, senseless evil.

In his years with NYPD, Haller had seen the darkest

sides of humanity. Gang violence, domestic murders, the occasional serial killer. But there was always a logic to it, twisted as it might be. Drugs, money, revenge, power. Something you could trace, understand, predict.

This wasn't that. It was calculated. Deliberate in its hate.

Lieberman finagled a pair of surgical gloves onto his chubby, doll-like hands. "Shall we?"

Haller gave a stiff nod, face flexing with rage. Lieberman cleared his throat, placed a set of readers over his tiny eyes, and thumbed through a manila folder to his report, gesturing and prodding accordingly as he read.

"Subject is Armstrong, Evelyn. Female. Eighteen years of age. Time of death occurred between 1:00 and 2:00 A.M., November 21st, 2022. Cause of death was via slit throat by a right-handed individual with a serrated knife. Left end of the injury started below the ear at the upper third of the neck and deepened gradually with severing of the left carotid artery before trailing off at the opposite side of the neck. Also evidence of asphyxiation prior to, possibly by the means of a leather belt. X-ray of the brain showed signs of swelling in conjunction with blunt force trauma to the scalp—"

"She was knocked out."

"And dragged, possibly uphill through rough terrain given the lacerations and abrasions on her legs. Ligature marks on her wrists and ankles, bound with quarter-inch rope. Right wrist was fractured entirely. Four-inch-wide laceration on her right bicep holding traces of..." He squinted. "Tree bark. Also evidence of vaginal intercourse with particularly malignant wounds consistent with rape. Suspect used a condom."

"Any prints?"

"Zero. And—"

Lieberman trailed off. Haller's eyebrows shot up.

"What?"

Lieberman folded his readers solemnly and shut the manila folder.

"She was pregnant, Sheriff. About eleven weeks."

Two lives stolen in one brutal act. The killer hadn't just murdered Evelyn. He'd erased an entire future. Some crimes were so complete in their destruction they defied comprehension. Haller felt the blood drain from his face. The two men shared something of a moment of silence. Just when Haller believed this couldn't possibly become more horrific—

Richard could never know.

Haller sucked his teeth. "I'll take the report."

Lieberman offered the folder. Haller went to grip it—

But Lieberman held on.

"My advice, Sheriff?"

Their eyes met. Surprise in Haller's, something spooked in Lieberman's.

"Call the FBI." The words carried weight beyond their syllables. An admission that whatever had come to Bronxville was beyond their small-town understanding. Some evil required federal intervention, the kind that crossed state lines and left trails of bodies in its wake.

As Haller left the morgue, the words echoed in his skull. Two girls missing in a month. One murdered. One still unaccounted for. Evelyn's death hadn't been impulsive. Not a crime of passion.

It was the kind of thing that didn't stop until someone made it.

Back in his patrol car, Haller pulled out a phone he hadn't used in years and dialed a number he hoped he'd never need.

The rest of the day passed in a trance.

He returned to his office, shut the door, closed the blinds.

The folder lay untouched on his desk.

For three hours, he sat there gnawing at yellowed fingertips, haunted.

Call the FBI.

Later that night, Maple Haller prepared her husband's favorite dish: short rib, mashed potatoes, and steamed vegetables.

It may as well have been gruel.

It wasn't like Haller to lug work home. But, even after forty years in law enforcement, this was unlike anything he'd ever seen, much less overseen.

And so he sat at the table, deeply stricken, as Maple went on about her day at the salon, peddling dime-store gossip to fill the air because, of course, did you hear about Margaret Foley's youngest? Early admission to Yale! Always was in the library, that one. And did you hear the Hawthorne's are divorcing? Ten years too late, if you ask me. Oh, and did you see what Barb did to her hair? *Heavens*!

Call the FBI.

The couple of thirty-five years took to bed at eight. Maple puttered with her hair done up in rollers. Haller stared endlessly at the cottage cheese ceiling.

"You believe in ghosts, M?" he suddenly asked.

She frowned. "Why do you ask, hon'?"

"No reason."

Outside, the first flurries began to fall over Bronxville. Light, hesitant, almost gentle. But the sky was turning. And what would come with the storm wasn't just cold.

It was something far worse.

Maple drifted off.

The old man could hear the cries now.

Roger Lopez was surprised to hear his son had no-called at the mill that Wednesday. Some of the guys smoking cigarettes in the break room joked that he must be off with some girl. He laughed it off. But deep down, he knew it was unlike his boy.

He blocked it out and pushed through his shift. Whatever it was, they'd crack a beer later and sort it out as they always did. They shared an enviable bond, underlined by a real compassion and understanding for one another, which had remained consistent in the years following the incident. They had each, of course, weathered an unfathomable tragedy early on in their respective lives. Roger had lost his wife. Frankie had lost his mother.

Roger had raised Frankie alone since he was nine, after the accident. He'd done his best, working double shifts at the mill to put food on the table, trying to be both mother and father to a boy whose grief habitually manifested as rage. He'd weathered Frankie's teenage years. The fights, the juvenile detentions, the rebellion. With a steadfast empathy born of his own loss.

And somehow, against all odds, they'd forged something good. Something solid. Frankie had graduated high school, gotten a job at the mill, seemed to be finding his way. Much of that, Roger believed, was due to Evelyn Armstrong. She'd seen something in his son that others missed. Something worth loving.

On his drive home, he stopped at a Sunoco and grabbed

a bag of Flamin' Hot Funyuns, two packs of Lucky Strike 100s, and a Diet Coke. Hell, he was already there. Rack of Miller Lites, too. They were running low.

He arrived back to the house at eight-thirty, another twelve-hour day under his belt. He walked inside, the floor creaking under his weight, and called for his son. Nothing.

He set the beer down on the counter and announced its presence. Still, nothing.

He marched the five yards to his son's bedroom, knocked twice, and opened the door.

A flurry of relief swept over the old man, but it was quickly extinguished by something else. His son was there, but... but...

The fuck was going on here?

Frankie was shirtless and sitting on the edge of his bed covered in sweat, convalescing from a night run with his eyes pointed at the ground and glistening with tears. *NEWS10 ABC* was running wrap-up segments on his thirty-six-inch TV. His father's brow creased.

"What's the matter, boy?"

Frankie finally met his father's eyes.

"I think I messed up really bad."

Roger crossed the room and sat beside his son, the bed sagging under their combined weight. On the screen, footage of Twin Lakes County Park played at a low volume, yellow police tape fluttering in the breeze.

"Evelyn?" Roger asked quietly.

Frankie nodded, tears streaming down his face. "They found her. In the woods."

"Jesus," Roger breathed. He placed a hand on his son's shoulder, feeling the tremors running through his body. "Frank, what happened?"

"I saw her," Frankie said, his voice breaking. "At the

party. I told her not to get in the car with Sarah. She was drunk. I knew it wasn't safe."

"That don't make this your fault."

"You don't understand, Pop. We had a fight. A couple weeks ago." Frankie wiped his eyes with the back of his hand. "She was pregnant."

Roger's grip on his son's shoulder tightened. "What?"

"She called me. Said she was gonna... get rid of it." Frankie's voice cracked. "I said terrible things to her. Things I can't take back."

"Frank—"

"And now she's dead." Frankie looked up at his father, his eyes red-rimmed and desperate. "She's dead and they're gonna think I did it. They're gonna think I killed her. They're gonna—"

Roger pulled his son into his arms instinctively, feeling him shake violently with sobs. "We'll figure this out," he said, not knowing what that even meant. "We'll get through this together."

The boy didn't answer. Just pressed his face into the wool lining of his father's coat and cried like a dying fawn. Small, shuddering, already slipping away.

Roger held on, listening to the broken sounds coming from a boy who never broke.

And beneath the grief, beneath the silence, something cold settled into his gut.

This wasn't over.

It hadn't even begun.

The Armstrong residence had been irreparably flipped upside down. The air was heavy, almost suffocating, with a quietness that was deafening. Phantoms of the past seemed to dart in the shadows of the Dutch Colonial before retreating to its darkened crevices. Less than a week ago, the lives of the Armstrongs had been going about their usual ordained cycles, for better or worse. That dynamic had since been clobbered into a billion microscopic shards, which would now lie excruciatingly and inescapably underfoot for the rest of time.

It was 9:30 P.M. Richard, hazy-eyed, stumbled about with a fifth of whiskey, the liquor lapping against the inside of the bottle with each restless torque of his pacing. Janet had taken sick to her bed with a steamer and a fistful of Klonopin, and for the last six hours had muddled through VHSs of Evelyn as a child through swollen, bloodshot eyes. The marathon had ended with the one on her ninth birthday, and the TV was now statically frozen on the face of young Evelyn, beaming beside her white cake with a pink birthday cap on.

Outside, news vans had begun to gather again, reporters speaking in hushed, respectful tones to the cameras. Neighbors had left flowers on the porch, casseroles in foil pans, cards expressing condolences that couldn't begin to touch their grief.

The phone had rung incessantly until Richard had yanked it from the wall. Janet's sister had arrived from Boston, taken one look at the state of them both, and quietly begun to manage the logistics that death demands. Funeral arrangements, obituary notices, calls to relatives. Things that required functioning when the bereaved could barely breathe.

Richard ambled up the stairs. He stopped at Evelyn's room. Zeus was curled up in a ball and whining on her bed.

Richard entered and went to pet him. On his way out, he stopped at the door, in which Evelyn's red Bronxville High hoodie hung. He buried his nose in it.

The scent of her (strawberry shampoo, a hint of vanilla) was still there, preserved in the fabric like a time capsule. He inhaled deeply, desperately, as if he could somehow pull her back to him through sheer force of will.

After a while, he checked on Janet, who was all but knocked out. He walked over to the TV and shut it off. He looked at Janet. She was on her side, tightly enveloped in the covers like a giant burrito, with her cloudy, despondent gaze facing out the window.

"You need anything, hon'?" he asked his wife.

She didn't respond. Richard took the cue and began to head for the door.

"Richard?" she croaked.

He turned back. "Yes?"

"Who would hurt our baby?

"I don't know, sweetie."

"Why couldn't we protect her?"

He inhaled deeply. "I don't know."

The words hung in the air between them, an indictment, a shared failure. They had one job. To keep their daughter safe. And they had failed.

"They'll find who did this," Janet whispered, her voice flat and distant. "Won't they?"

"Yes," Richard said with a certainty that surprised even him. "They will."

Whether it would be the police or himself, Richard didn't say. But in that moment, as he looked at his broken wife, at the ruins of their life together, he made a silent promise to Evelyn.

He would find who did this. And they would pay. The

promise tasted like blood and gunpowder on his tongue. Richard had killed before. Clean kills, sanctioned by flag and country. But this would be different. This would be personal. This would be slow.

He went back downstairs. Took a swig. Broke wind. And then stumbled into his office. He grabbed a blanket hanging off his chair, flicked the lamp off, and collapsed into his awful couch, pulling the throw up to his chin.

Though, hard as he tried, there was no sleep for him.

He could hear the grandfather clock tick in the living room.

And tick.

Richard awoke Thanksgiving Day to reporters hounding his property. CNN, FOX, NBC, the *Times*—all swarming like buzzards and blocking the road with their vans, each waiting for the slightest of movement within to start firing off their bulbs.

It was 10:00 A.M. Richard, terribly hungover and pale-eyed, rolled off the sofa and onto his knees with a displeasured groan and a crack. He crawled to peer through the slits of the blinds. *Yep*, went through his mind lazily. *That's the press alright.*

He pulled them shut completely, blanketing him in darkness. Still, he quickly located the bottle.

The house itself was silent. Upstairs, Janet still hadn't emerged from their bedroom. This was supposed to be their first Thanksgiving with Evelyn home from college. Janet had planned a feast. Turkey with all the trimmings, Evelyn's favorite pumpkin pie, her signature stuffing recipe, the good china that only came out for holidays. Now the ingredients sat untouched in the refrigerator.

Richard's cell rang. He patted his pockets, then his thighs, found it on the armrest, and slid into the old leather swivel chair.

Picked up without checking.

"Hey, Dick, it's Haller," the sheriff said, guilt coating every word. "Happy Thanksgiving,"

"Sheriff."

Richard popped the cork on the whiskey bottle, grabbed a clean glass from the drawer, and poured two fingers. The line hummed in the silence, until—

"How you holding up, Dick?" Haller asked, wincing as the words left his mouth. He was the only man in the office that Thursday morning, wearing a worn jean jacket over black jeans and a flannel that had seen too many winters. Working a few hours on Thanksgiving had become something of a ritual. Maple handled the last-minute shopping, and he came in to "clear the decks," as he always called it. In truth, he liked the stillness. The emptiness of the office, the hum of the heater, the way the paperwork didn't talk back. It gave him an excuse to drink coffee from a chipped mug and pretend the world outside wasn't all noise and unfinished business. A quiet morning. A few signatures. Cigarette with the window open. Then he'd go home, carve the bird, and act like the weight in his chest had nothing to do with missing sleep and everything to do with Maple's stuffing.

But as soon as Richard answered his call that morning, he knew he should've called the stunt off this year.

Richard took a sip of whiskey. Let it burn. "I'm having a drink, Sheriff," Richard said.

"Right," Haller said, then cleared his throat. "Well, look, Dick... the autopsy report came in."

"And?"

"Cause of death was the throat wound. But there was... Ain't no easy way to say this, Dick. There was some—well, a lot of evidence suggesting prolonged assault prior to death." Haller paused, choosing his words carefully. "Extreme assault, Dick."

"How long had she been alive for?"

Fuck. Haller cleared his throat. "Twenty-four hours, Dick."

Richard's jaw set hard, like something locked behind it. A vein rose slowly along his temple, pulsing beneath the skin. He blinked once. Slowly. Then again, longer this time, like he was willing the world to reset when his eyes opened.

But it didn't. It wouldn't.

His fingers tightened around the glass, just enough to make it creak.

"Suspects?" he asked, voice dry and flat, like his throat had been scraped clean.

"We're looking. But I need to be straight with you, Dick. This doesn't happen in Bronxville. We're a small department. You know this."

"What are you saying?"

"I'm saying we're doing our best," Haller said. It came out more defensive than he'd intended. "Let us do our job."

"Yeah? Why don't you try doing some fucking work then?"

Richard hung up.

He sat motionless in that chair for the next hour, the sheriff's words echoing in his mind like some twisted anti-mantra. Twenty-four hours. While he'd been passed out, drunk and drooling with his mouth open to the ceiling fan, writing some shitty article about a shitty parade peddled by a shitty—

A realization settled in his gut like a crash landing.

Jarring at first, hard and blunt.

Then it *spread*. Slow and warm, like opium splitting into the bloodstream.

Strong. Intoxicating.

Irreversible.

Trance-like, he rose and made his way to the cabinet above the fridge where he kept his gun safe. The combination came to him automatically. Evelyn's birthday. The safe opened with a soft *click* to reveal his service pistol—a SIG Sauer P226, matte black, worn smooth at the grip from years of use. He picked it up gently, like it might still be asleep. Checked the chamber, the magazine, the slide. Everything was right where it should be.

Richard stood there a moment, the weight of the gun in his hand and something heavier blooming in his chest.

Not rage. Not grief.

Resolution.

Some decisions arrived like lightning. Sudden, brilliant, irreversible. Others grew like cancer, spreading through your consciousness until they became the only truth that mattered. Richard felt both happening at once, duty and darkness converging into something that felt like destiny.

Outside, the reporters waited, cameras ready.

Inside, Richard Armstrong tried something new.

PART TWO

PRINCE

CHAPTER NINE

PRINCE

NOVEMBER 27, 2022

It was a brisk morning in Manhattan. Fog curled at the edges of Central Park, muting the blaze of red, orange, and yellow. The city was still finding its noise as Special Agent James Prince pushed through his 8:00 A.M. run, gray sweatshirt dark with sweat, stride cutting clean through the damp air.

He was a handsome man—six feet even, lean, with light Black skin and piercing green eyes, a gaze both driven and haunted. Morning runs were ritual, a habit since Harvard, when he'd rise in the dorms no later than 6:00 A.M., knock out five miles, then replace a quarter of the calories with two ham-and-cheese sandwiches and a black coffee—two sugars, no cream—from Simon's, which would be packed and sweltering with students and foul-mouthed construction workers alike by 8:00 A.M. every morning like—well, literally—like clockwork.

Five miles. He scoffed at it now. At thirty-seven, Prince didn't so much feel old yet as he *did not feel young*. Still, running helped Prince think, process.

He was born in Quantico, Virginia in 1985 to Michael Prince, an FBI agent, and Carmela Waters, an Italian-American desk clerk. His father had been one of the pioneers behind the FBI's groundbreaking Behavior Analysis Unit in the late 1970's, an elite serial killer profiling division designed to study psychopaths. From a young age, he wittingly mirrored his father's all-consuming fascination with the macabre and dark psychology. By the age of thirteen, he would regularly wait for his father to retire to his bedroom in order to tiptoe down into the living room with a flashlight and bury his nose unmolested in any and all files the old man may have lugged home on a particular night. He read forensic reports cover to cover, devoured steno interviews, studied photographs. When his father fought to rouse him in the mornings, he attributed it to those goddamn computer games, until one night when he finally caught him, and became furious. However, his anger subsided, and he began to take his son to the facility on weekends. Prince was overjoyed.

Other kids had superheroes; Prince had serial killers. Berkowitz, Rader, Manson, Speck, Kemper, Hance, Bundy, Gacy, Watts, Dahmer. Prince knew them all, from their origin to their methods to their capture. He never felt like a freak, and while it may have been worrisome if it were a traditional fixation, it was purely intellectual. It just interested him. Some are drawn to the predators of the jungle, and some to the ones of civilization.

His father had taught him to think like the hunters if

you want to catch them. To understand their pathology, their motivations, the dark logic that drove them.

At Harvard, Prince majored in Criminal Justice and mastered in Sociology. It was in this time that he met and began dating law student Tina Bolton, daughter of wealthy Massachusetts real estate magnate Matthew Bolton. Upon completion of his master's at the green age of twenty-four, Prince moved to New York and joined the New York Police Department while Tina embarked on her final year of law school in Cambridge. The two remained close, seeing each other whenever feasible. After a short year, Tina slam dunked the Bar and joined Prince in the city to begin a junior associate position at one of Manhattan's largest commercial firms. Nearly simultaneously, she discovered that she was pregnant.

Prince proposed immediately, and they married in Long Island in the January of 2011. For their wedding present, Tina's father gifted them a preserved 1899 brownstone in Brooklyn. Five months later, they welcomed a little girl: Zoe. The preceding fall, Prince made detective, and four idyllic years followed.

Those had been the golden years. Career on the rise, beautiful wife, perfect daughter, a home in Brooklyn that was the envy of his colleagues. From the outside, James Prince had it all.

Inside was a different story. With each solved case, Prince drifted further in, lost in the darkness he hunted. Faces of victims. The eerily friendly cadences of killers that don't match their empty eyes. And somewhere beneath it all, he knew the truth:

It had never been about justice. It was a game of proximity. How close he could get to evil before it recognized him.

Prince joined the FBI at thirty and immediately hit the ground running, exhibiting a rare poise and unteachable intuition. In just his third year in Violent Crimes, Prince solved The Metro Killer case. A 44-year-old janitor from Staten Island named Lucas Miller had been robbing, raping, and murdering women with a .44 Magnum in the subways, racking up five victims across a four-month run. While pursuing a new lead, he and partner Christopher Wilbur matched DNA from a half-eaten slice of pizza in Brooklyn to genetic material found on the remains of 46-year-old paralegal and mother of three Margaret Stevenson, and Miller was arrested. Overnight, Prince became a rockstar.

It could be said that manifestations of destiny, while divine, arrive with unwritten contingencies, often involving conscious or subconscious sacrifices. Prince viewed his job more so as a craft, one to be nurtured and perpetually scrutinized, and so he, much like his father before him, became consumed. He began to neglect Tina, sexually and emotionally; arrive home grossly late; and flat-out miss birthdays. He also developed a drinking habit, and it was that first sting of liquor by the kitchen counter after a day spent buried in evidence which would quietly supersede the warm embrace of his counterpart at the door. The bottle never asked questions, never demanded explanations for the darkness he carried home. It didn't care about the photographs burned into his memory or the voices of killers that echoed in his sleep. Alcohol was the only partner that understood his work completely.

Nevertheless, Prince continued to soar professionally, and it could not be denied that his trajectory had been enviable.

His talents garnered considerable attention from superiors and colleagues alike, one of whom was a lively thirty-year-old profiler named Jennifer Nielsen. Their collaboration on cases evolved into late-night sessions together, and eventually, rounds at The Plaza Hotel.

It came to a head in the June of 2021 after a full year of hiding when Prince attempted to sneak in one night at 3:00 A.M. reeking of alcohol and expensive perfume, just a week after his thirty-sixth birthday. Tina had waited up in the den to confront him. He accepted his fate, and his wife of ten years filed for divorce the following day. It was finalized within four months.

He sustained his relationship with Jennifer. The two went in together on a condo in Midtown, and now—

It was Sunday, and a perfect morning for a run despite the whiskey from last night—and four slices of a large pizza from Remo's—still sloshing around in his belly. Cyclists and joggers traversed the salted paths alongside him, with canvas painters basking in the crisp tranquility of the sprawling park, young couples laying out idyllically in the soft grass with their kids—

Hold on. Kids. Fuck.

And Sunday. Double fuck.

Tonight was his night with Zoe. Specifically, tonight was the night he'd finally have to explain to his eleven-year-old daughter why his seat at Thanksgiving had been empty. He worried less about facing Tina and her petulant scowl. Sure, she'd be pissed. About as predictable as the Giants collapsing by halftime.

The whole anxiety of the thing was humorously ironic to Prince. In his seven years in Violent Crimes, he'd interviewed, examined, interrogated, and even broken bread with dozens upon dozens of serial killers, rapists, child murderers, and the like without ever so much as breaking a sweat, but it would be a ninety-pound little girl with pigtails who implanted the very fear of God into his stomach time after time.

Pancakes for dinner. That always worked.

When she was nine, at least.

He came to a stop by a bench under a maple, propping a leg up and holding his hips (okay, now he felt old) with sweat beaming down his face as he gulped cold air with mortal desperation.

A cool breeze sighed through the trees.

One mile would do it today.

On Tuesday, he and Wilbur would drive Upstate to Bronxville to meet with the local sheriff and begin piecing together what had happened to a girl named Evelyn Armstrong. It would be the usual routine. Establish a base of operations, review the evidence, interview witnesses, build a profile of both victim and killer.

As he headed back to his apartment to shower before picking up Zoe, a sort of dread settled in his stomach. The kind he only felt when facing the worst of the worst. The ones who killed not out of passion or greed or rage, but out of some perverse, internal logic that made sense only to them.

True predators. The ones who hunt for sport until they're put down.

Some cases announced themselves. Media circuses, political pressure, obvious motives. Others arrived quietly, wrapped in small-town tragedy, carrying a malevolence that felt almost biblical in its scope.

This felt like the latter.

Prince left his bureau sedan running as he crossed the tree-lined street to his old Brooklyn home, the preserved 1899 brownstone with oversized windows and—sigh—a grand staircase. A casualty of the divorce, naturally, and one which he still quietly grieved.

It was 5:50 P.M., so Tina certainly couldn't rag on him for lateness. He flew up the steps past the ajar gate, wearing a black Members Only jacket over a gray T-shirt, and knocked thrice.

Bustling. Shouting. He braced. Tiny footsteps descended the staircase, then became closer and shorter until the door finally clacked and groaned open to reveal Zoe.

She'd grown since he'd last seen her, just two weeks ago. Or maybe it was the way she carried herself—less like a child, more like a young woman beginning to test the boundaries of independence. Her dark curly hair was pulled back in a neat ponytail, and she wore jeans and a purple sweater he didn't recognize. She had his eyes—the same intense green—but Tina's delicate features, her smile.

"Hi, Dad."

"Hi, pumpkin. You ready?"

Tina darkened the doorway, one hand resting lightly on Zoe's shoulder. She wore a black dress and heels that complemented her cocoa skin and straightened hair, polished to a mirror sheen. A date, he assumed. She'd worn the same with him. "Get your backpack, sweetie."

Prince gave a nod of reassurance to his daughter, and she scurried back inside.

And then there were two.

Their eyes met. There was that scowl.

"You look nice," Prince offered, diplomatic.

"Where were you on Thanksgiving?"

Straight to it. And in that cutting lawyer tone of hers. Fine.

"I was with Jennifer at her parents' in Hoboken," Prince said, then decided to double down with a classic. "Not that it's any of your business."

"Unfortunately, it becomes my business when our daughter is crying in my bed and asking why daddy doesn't love her because you'd rather run away with your mistress."

The words stung.

"I'm sorry." He really was.

"She doesn't need apologies," Tina said, voice low. "She needs her father. Present. Consistent." Her eyes narrowed. "Sober."

The accusation hung between them like smoke from a gun. Tina had always been surgical with her words, able to find the exact pressure point that would make him bleed. She knew his weaknesses better than he did, had watched him catalog them over ten years of marriage.

Prince stiffened. "Tina—"

"New case?"

"What?"

"I see it in your eyes. Lookin' like a motherfucker on 67th who just took a hit. What is it now? Quadruple-rape, Ted Bundy's twin?"

"To be fair, I asked if Jennifer and I could come together, and you shot it down."

"I don't *want* that bitch in my house, James—"

Zoe returned to the door in her pink JanSport with

Tina's rebound Brian Townley, an ICU nurse with Mount Sinai, at her heels.

Tina held her tongue. "Back by nine. Good luck."

"Don't need it," he said as she shredded off, her heels clicking off the walls of the foyer. He smiled at Zoe. "Got your homework?"

"Yep," she muttered, blowing past him and skipping down the steps, backpack bobbing, to wait by the gate.

"How you doin', James?" Townley said, adjusting the cuff links on his white shirt. He was a large man, a brawny six-four, with shoulders like a bison and a bald torpedo of a head. He and Tina had met earlier in the year when Zoe had fallen off the jungle gym at lunch and broken her wrist. He'd set it, provided them with extra antibiotics, and bought them dinner. He was a good man, one who elicited charm and magnanimity in droves, with a brilliant smile and gentle blue eyes that exuded ease and warmth even to a reptile like Prince.

He wanted to hate him. God, he wanted to hate him.

"Fine, Brian," he said, keeping one eye on Zoe below.

"Missed you at Thanksgiving."

"That's what I hear."

"Look, don't worry about Tina," Brian whispered. "She's got a lot on her mind with this case she just took on. And, trust me, Zoe's already forgotten about it. She's been talking about tonight all weekend."

He really, really wanted to hate him. But hatred required energy Prince didn't possess, emotion he'd spent on darker pursuits. Brian was a reminder of the man he might have been in another life—one where he'd chosen healing over hunting, where he'd learned to build instead of tear apart.

"You got a special young lady right there," he said. "Have fun."

"Thanks, Brian."

"No problem."

He closed the door.

Prince stared at the closed door for a moment, fighting the familiar mixture of resentment and self-loathing. Brian was everything he wasn't—steady, present, reliable. The kind of man who showed up when he said he would. The kind who didn't lose himself in bottles or murder cases or other women. And he loved Jennifer. But Tina was his Achilles heel. Always would be. Which is why he had to ruin it.

He pushed the thought away as he descended the steps to join his daughter. She was watching a squirrel dart across the yard, her face lit with simple, childlike fascination. For a moment, Prince saw her as she had been at four, at five, at six—before the late nights and missed recitals and eventual divorce had cast their shadow over her childhood.

Prince and Zoe took up a booth in New Daisy's Diner. He ordered the lumberjack pancakes for the table—enough for five—and shared with her. At a quarter to seven, she hoisted her backpack up to the seat, zipped it open, and dropped a binder on the table. For thirty minutes, they worked on her homework in the semi-gloom of the diner, which proved to be a breeze for her and a challenge to him, and at 7:30—

"Honey, can I talk to you about something?"

"Sure," she replied, still picking at the pancakes.

"It's about Thanksgiving."

"I know you were with Jennifer," she said wisely, mouth

full. "Don't worry about it. I like her."

"Okay."

"My turn," she said, setting her silverware aside. "Do you think you and Mommy will get back together?"

"I don't know, honey."

"I think she misses you," she said, with the kind of gentle unawareness only a child could have. Before they learn what adults mean when they talk about love. Before they know how beautiful and devastating and thrilling and unimaginably complicated it can be. "Brian's cool, but he's gone a lot. Sometimes when he works nights, I hear her crying in her room."

Prince felt a sting in his gut. His eyes dropped to the table. He could feel them start to sink. Flat and gray, like old pennies tossed into a well.

What's that saying about telling the truth? Crazy people and children are the only ones who do? Adults learned to lie by omission, to smile through devastation, to carry secrets like tumors. Children hadn't developed that particular cancer yet. They spoke the truth because they didn't know it could be weaponized.

Zoe went back to her plate, humming faintly through her nose like the conversation hadn't just detonated. Because she didn't know.

Kids were like that. Resilient, oblivious, brutal in their honesty.

He stared at the wood grain in the table and thought about how many times he'd let Tina cry behind a door, and how many times he'd pretended not to hear it.

Not out of cruelty.

He didn't know what.

"Can we have another movie night with Jennifer soon?" Zoe transitioned.

Prince snapped out of it. “Yeah, sure, honey. We can do that.”

She beamed at him, all forgiveness and second chances. Children had that capacity. To love wholly and without reservation, even when you failed them.

Especially when you failed them.

Prince reached across the table and squeezed her hand. “I’m sorry I wasn’t there, Zo. I’m going to do better, okay?”

She shrugged, already moving on. “It’s okay, Dad. I saved you some pumpkin pie. It’s in my backpack.”

Something cracked in Prince’s chest. A fissure in the wall he’d built around his emotions. He swallowed hard against the sudden lump in his throat.

“Thanks, baby.”

The morning of November 28th, 2022, began like any other.

Prince roused at 6:00 A.M. beside Jennifer, who was face down in a black tank top with her blonde hair strewn wildly across their gray silk pillows. He lumbered into the kitchen in his briefs with a prominent erection and sleepily slapped together the ingredients for his usual breakfast smoothie: quarter splash of almond milk, scoop of chocolate protein powder, frozen blueberries, one banana, an egg, a couple godforsaken dates from the bottom drawer of the fridge, and a serving of almond butter. At 6:15, he slipped on his sweatsuit and running shoes, put a pot of coffee on, and floated three stories down to their fitness center, where he lifted free weights for a half hour on the dot before embarking on a light run around Midtown.

When he arrived back home, Jennifer was up and straightening her hair. He slapped her on the ass and jumped into the shower, and then got dressed (black suit with an open-collar gray shirt), gave her a kiss, filled his black Thermos with the coffee since brewed, and took the elevator down to the stuffy parking garage. A Marlboro lit, he slipped behind the wheel and headed for the facility.

By the time he stepped onto the dull carpet of the Violent Crimes floor, not five seconds passed before Special Agent Christopher Wilbur, his partner of nearly seven years, came barreling up to him.

"Morning, handsome," Wilbur said, grinning. "Cochran wants us in his office."

"Were you waiting by the elevator?"

"No. Maybe. Yes."

"What's it about? Bronxville?"

"Gotta be," Wilbur said, already turning.

They moved briskly down the corridor.

Wilbur was trim, clean-cut, and maybe an inch shorter than Prince. They'd come up through the ranks together. Two rookies turned inseparable, now veterans with a case file count in the dozens. Their partnership worked because it shouldn't have: Wilbur was breezy, charming, and self-effacing. Prince carried the weight of every room he walked into. Wilbur went slow. Prince ran hot. And only one of them could shake hands without starting an internal affairs investigation.

They stopped outside the frosted glass door of New York FBI Director Raylan Cochran's office.

"Come in," came Cochran's voice from inside, flat and immediate.

Prince opened the door, Wilbur at his flank.

Cochran sat behind a wide mahogany desk, a man who looked like he'd been carved from scotch, steak, and second chances. Late sixties, frosted hair, dark eyes. The kind that didn't miss much. His pressed white shirt and black suspenders clung to a body padded over the years by long hours and late dinners, but he wore it all with authority. His circle glasses magnified the stare of a man who'd seen more than he'd report, and done more than he'd admit.

The office smelled of burnt coffee, boxed cigars, and something like slow-burning rage.

"Sit," he said, not looking up from his paperwork.

They did.

He finished his signature with a flick of a Montblanc, set it aside, then leaned back in his chair and looked them both over.

"Gentlemen," he said, removing his readers and resting them on a stack of case files. "Figured I'd give you a primer on the Upstate fiasco before you pack your lunchboxes. You two look it over?"

"A bit," Prince said.

"Watched the news segment," Wilbur added. "Most of my intel came from my wife's Facebook feed, though."

"Evelyn Armstrong," Cochran said, ignoring the joke and folding his hands. "Second young lady to disappear in the greater Eastchester area this month. Only this time, after three days..."

Cochran tossed a manila folder to Prince, who immediately wet his thumb and dove in.

"...they found her, ravaged and discarded in Twin Lakes County Park," Cochran said. "Sheriff's department says she was last seen leaving her friend's car following a little party."

Prince's moistened thumb stopped on the photo of her

face taken at the scene, and for a moment he marveled morbidly at the simultaneous ferocity and clinical precision in which her throat had been cut. Immediately, he knew this was no one-off, no run-in, no accident. This was not the work of a drifter or some rogue psycho, but of a prideful, capable monster; calculated, deliberate, and uniformly vicious.

A rare chill befell him. This wasn't the familiar cold of a crime scene or the clinical detachment of forensic evidence. This was recognition. The uncomfortable certainty that he was looking at the work of someone who understood violence the way a composer understood music.

"She was the eighteen-year-old daughter of a local figure and veteran. A student. Her death has created a bit of a stir in the town."

Prince flipped to the coroner's report and began to skim key words. *Ligature marks... lacerations... fractured wrist... consistent with rap*e—

"Any suspects at this time?" Prince asked, eyes downcast.

"None," Cochran said flatly. "You're to leave in the morning tomorrow. Your contact in the SD is one Joseph Haller. He'll get you up to speed."

Prince shared a look with Wilbur, then shut the file and met Cochran's stare as if to confirm that that was all.

"Upstate is beautiful this time of year, gentlemen," Cochran concluded. "Go catch yourselves a killer."

The two nodded and rose.

As he was walking out of the office, Prince felt a strange feeling come over him, one which he couldn't quite identify. Like, despite all his wit, acumen, and years of experience in the field, he was walking into something bad. Some cases solved themselves. Others were labyrinths designed by minds that thought three moves ahead. Prince felt the weight of the maze before he'd even entered it.

He shook it off.

An oil painting depicting the Bay of Pigs hung by the door.

CHAPTER TEN

BE CAREFUL

Prince took the afternoon to drop groceries off at his mother's. In the last year, he'd moved her up from Quantico to a two-bedroom, ground-level condo in Greenwich, where she filled her twilight days with (in this order) gardening, magazine clipping, feeding the neighborhood strays, sewing in the spare bedroom, reruns of *Let's Make a Deal*, and Stoli. Lots and lots of Stoli.

He dropped the paper bags, fat with non-perishables and cat food, on the kitchen table as Carmela Prince smoked a Pall Mall by the sink in a Japanese robe, in a bit of a daze as she basked in a stream of sun. She was full-blooded Sicilian, and at nearly seventy was aging quite well, contrary to the eighty-proof empties which lined her counters. Her jet-black hair held just the slightest streaks of silver, and her skin seemed to boast an eternal glow. Her eyes were green like her son's, but kinder (and drunker).

Prince reached into one of the bags, withdrew a handle of Stoli, and set it down on the table with a thump. He wondered how such a tiny old woman could drink so prolifically. Like, *really* wondered.

"Have you seen your father lately?" she asked from across the kitchen, ashing the Pall Mall in the sink.

"Been busy," Prince mumbled.

Yeah, real busy. The last three months had been the slowest in his entire career.

"You should see your father." She opened a cabinet and pulled out two glasses.

Prince ignored her. It had been a year now since Michael Prince had gotten dementia and been hauled off to a specialized Senior Living in New Haven. The last time he'd trekked to see the old man, he hadn't recognized Prince. Not even a little. Actually, he'd mistaken him for an orderly, worked himself up into a biblical lather over a piece of lint on the floor. The truth was, Prince didn't avoid visiting his father because he was busy, or because he didn't love him. He avoided it because it broke his heart. Some losses arrived slowly, stripping away recognition piece by piece until the person you loved was only a stranger wearing their face. Prince had spent his entire career studying minds that snapped clean. Nothing compared to the slow erasure of his hero.

Carmela walked over with the glasses and set them down by the jug of Stoli. She cracked the seal, lifted it with two trembling hands, and tilted at least two shots into each.

"I'm fine, Ma—"

"Just have a drink with your mother," she snapped in Italian.

Prince sighed and sat down. He picked up his glass,

clinked it with hers, and knocked it back with a face.

"How are you and Tina?"

"Still divorced, Ma."

"Awful business." She lit another Pall Mall.

Prince twirled his glass on the table as his mother smoked, the scent of the vodka numbing his nostrils.

Carmela studied her son, seeing beyond his composure to the darkness gathering behind his eyes. She'd seen that look before, in her husband's face when a case consumed him. It had always signaled trouble ahead.

"New case?" she asked, her accent thickening with concern.

Prince nodded, not meeting her gaze. "Girl murdered upstate. Maybe a serial."

She muttered a prayer in Italian. "You be careful, my love. Some monsters, they like when you hunt them. That's how they get a piece of you."

Prince felt the juvenile impulse to argue, to tell her he was a professional who knew what he was doing. To laugh it off, to hide behind the badge. But they both knew that had nothing to do with it. Professionalism meant nothing when what you hunted wanted you just as badly.

He could feel the slow erosion already. How each case chipped away at something essential, leaving him harder, colder, more distant from the people he loved. His marriage had crumbled under the weight of it all, his relationship with Zoe strained by absences both physical and emotional. He was becoming a collection of these absences, defined more by what he'd lost than what remained.

Three little girls were hula hooping on a neighboring lawn when Prince left his mothers, and climbed back into his bureau sedan. It was 3:40 P.M.

He twisted the key into the ignition and fired up the

Ford. He sat there for a moment, staring ahead blankly to the idle hum of the engine and muted ambiance of laughing children. That strange sensation he'd felt while exiting Cochran's office had returned, and uglily. It was of a gnawing sort, which seemed to crawl up his spine and perch tauntingly at the nape of his neck. Was it nerves? Perhaps he hadn't asked enough questions. Certainly, it wasn't fear.

Certainly not. Fear was for civilians, for people who didn't understand that monsters were just broken humans with broken impulses. But this felt different. Not fear of the killer, but fear of himself. Fear of how far he might go to catch this one, what lines he might cross in the name of justice.

Maybe it was nerves. He hadn't asked enough questions. Yes, that's what it was. After all, he hadn't worked much in the last few months. He'd gotten comfortable. *Too* comfortable. The nerves would wane. They always did. He just needed to get started, that's all.

Without thinking, he dug out his cell and dialed Tina. The impulse surprised him. Somewhere in his subconscious, she remained his anchor, the voice that could pull him back from the edge when cases threatened to consume him entirely. Even divorced, even with Brian in her bed, she was still the one he called when the darkness felt too heavy.

"Hello?"

He adjusted his posture and cleared his throat. "Hey, it's James."

"Hey, I'm at work. What's wrong?"

"Nothing," he quickly assured, and cleared his throat again. He could hear the phones in the background. "I just wanted to let you know that I'm going to be headed out of town for a bit."

"How long?"

"Not sure."

"You have Zoe this weekend!"

"I know."

"Well, where are you going?"

"Bronxville. I took a case."

"Evelyn Armstrong?"

"How'd you know?"

"How wouldn't I? It's all over the place. It's awful, James. Really, really awful. God, her poor parents..."

"Yeah, well, I'm going to see if I can't find the son of a bitch that did it."

The line went silent.

"You there?"

"Yeah." They both took a pause now, then Tina said, "Well, good luck."

"Thanks."

"And James?"

He felt a rare tremble in her voice. "Yeah?"

"Be careful. These are bad people."

Bad didn't begin to cover it. Prince had learned to categorize evil. Opportunistic, pathological, circumstantial. But some killers transcended category, operating from a logic so alien it defied profiling. Those were the ones who left investigators hollow, changed, carrying pieces of their madness long after the case closed.

The words hung between them, laden with history and unspoken fears. They'd had this conversation before, at the start of cases that had nearly consumed him. Cases that had led to missed dinners, forgotten anniversaries, and eventually, other women's beds.

"I will," he promised, knowing it might be a lie.

As he hung up, Prince watched the girls with their hula hoops, their laughter drifting through his open window. Their innocence, their safety, was what he fought for. What he sacrificed for.

But sometimes he wondered if the price was too high.

Prince spent his last night home watching a movie and eating ice cream with Jennifer. A bottle of red wine sat breathing in the center of the glass coffee table.

They'd been on a silent film binge. Tonight, it was *Nosferatu*.

"Why do I always eat junk when I'm with you?" Prince asked, shoveling another spoonful of mint chocolate chip into his mouth.

She giggled. "Sure. Blame me."

He smiled, but it faded quick. "I don't know about this one."

"I told you we should've gotten the Rocky Road."

"I mean the case."

She set her bowl down on the table and looked at him. "What's on your mind?"

"A valedictorian. Brutally murdered in her hometown of six thousand, and not *one* suspect? It's unthinkable. Small-town incompetence is one thing, but this? This is blindness."

Or willful ignorance. Prince had seen it before. Communities so desperate to preserve their illusion of safety they'd overlook obvious suspects, rationalize away evidence, protect their own even when their own were predators. Evil thrived in places that refused to acknowledge its existence.

"Drifter?"

"No. Rings too personal. Whoever it was, she knew him. She probably trusted him. Might've even looked up to him once."

He swapped the ice cream for the wine, poured a glass, and leaned back.

"But here's what I know," he said. "Somebody's killing girls up there. Getting away with it. And that I can't have. Right now, he's just a face in the crowd."

On the screen, Orlok stared back through grain and shadow.

Prince met his gaze.

"And all I need is to look him in the eye."

That was Prince's gift and his curse. The ability to see past facades, to recognize the predator behind the friendly smile. But recognition came with a price. Once you'd stared into that kind of darkness, it stared back. Once you understood how monsters thought, you couldn't unknow it.

Jennifer watched him, recognizing the familiar intensity that signaled the beginning of his descent into a case. She'd seen it before. The way his focus narrowed, his world contracting until there was nothing but the hunt. It both attracted and frightened her.

"Just don't lose yourself in this one," she said softly, touching his arm. "Come back to me."

Prince covered her hand with his, offering a smile that didn't reach his eyes. "Always do, don't I?"

But they both knew the truth. Each time he went away, a little less of him returned. The job was vampiric, feeding on empathy and innocence until you became something else entirely. Prince wondered sometimes if the difference between him and the killers he hunted was just timing. Whether he'd simply chosen the legal outlet for his particular brand of obsession with human darkness.

On the screen, Orlok's hollow eyes stared back through grain and shadow.

CHAPTER ELEVEN

A FACE IN THE CROWD

NOVEMBER 29, 2022

Prince and Wilbur hit the road at 8:30 A.M.

Traffic was dense, and it would amount to a forty-five-minute trip on the 9A. Wilbur's wife had sent him off with a buttered bagel, twelve-ounce Red Bull, and a roll of Mixed Fruit Mentos. Prince, manning the wheel, stuck to his Marlboro Lights and black coffee. They'd each packed a second suit and a set of gym clothes, and the agency had booked them adjoining rooms at the Westchester Lodge, a two-star no-tell shit heap held together by used condoms and only fiscally upright via the souls of the damned. Prince had honestly thought Cochran was joking upon looking it up.

Nope.

Prince had stayed in worse places. Safe houses in Detroit,

surveillance motels in Newark. But there was something about doing it on the bureau's dime that felt like punishment. Or maybe Cochran's way of reminding them this wasn't a glamour case, just another dead girl in a small town that thought money could buy safety.

Fifteen minutes in, Wilbur dusted the bagel off his hands, to which Prince winced, and cracked the Red Bull. He took a large gulp, smacked loudly, and sighed. Prince winced again.

"What's the first order of business?" Wilbur asked, setting the Red Bull down in the cupholder.

"We connect with the sheriff's department," Prince said. "Shake hands. Show face. Lay roots. Then I want to talk to the father."

"I hear he's been holed up."

"We'll get to him."

Prince drew a cigarette from his breast pocket and lit it, the smoke filling the car as they sped toward Bronxville.

Prince parked beside a lamppost in front of the Bronxville Sheriff's Department. The building was neoclassical, built of red brick and white-painted timber, with a ring of northern red oaks hemming it in.

He and Wilbur felt the sharp bite of cold on their necks as they stepped out of the sedan. Winter was unmistakably in bloom. The leaves of the red oaks lay scattered across the neatly-attended lawn, the trees now stark silhouettes of their former selves.

It was 9:30 A.M.

They breezed through the front doors, badges and

smiles out, and passed the receptionist (a middle-aged Black woman named Eleanor Smith) into the main office: windowless, filled with brown cubicles. The walls were tan. The tufted carpet, a worn cream.

Prince locked onto Deputy Marcus Nichols, hunched at his keyboard in a black short-sleeved shirt, coffee steaming at his elbow. A tiny dog (something fluffy and brown, barely bigger than the mug) dozed in his lap, its head bobbing with every keystroke.

Nichols brought the dog to work too often, but no one in the department had the heart to tell him not to.

"FBI," Prince said briskly. "We're here to make contact with Sheriff Haller."

Nichols paled. "Shit. What'd he do?"

Wilbur chuckled.

"We aren't here to arrest him, kid," Prince said, suppressing a smirk. He extended a hand. "James Prince. This is my partner, Special Agent Christopher Wilbur. We were called in on a case."

Nichols shifted carefully, trying not to wake the dog as he stood. He shook both their hands. "Deputy Nichols. You here about the Armstrong girl?"

"I'm sure we'll cross paths, Deputy. For now, we need to speak to the sheriff. Can you point us in his direction?"

Nichols gestured toward a glass cube at the far end of the room. "Sure thing."

"Thank you."

Wilbur glanced down at the dog, grinning. "Cute pup. Boy or girl?"

Nichols lit up. "Girl. Her name's Biscuit."

Wilbur gave a little wave and dropped his voice to a playful coo. "Hey there, Biscuit."

The dog snored softly.

Prince was already walking. The door to the office was ajar, but he still knocked.

"Sheriff Haller? Special Agents James Prince and Christopher Wilbur, Violent Crimes Division, Manhattan FBI. May we enter?"

"Please," Haller said.

Prince pushed the door open. Haller sat behind his desk, landline to his ear. He held up a finger, gestured toward the two wool accent chairs ahead of the desk. Prince and Wilbur sat.

"Yes, honey... Just take him out before you leave... Yes, he ate... Okay, I love you... Have a good day at work... Okay, bye."

He hung up. "The wife."

Prince nodded. "Understood."

"You must be Prince," Haller said, standing and offering a handshake. "You two get in okay?"

"Bit of traffic. Nothing unusual."

"You ever been out this way?"

Prince cut the smile. "Sheriff, with the greatest respect: a girl's been dead a week and two days. Can we skip the country niceties and get to it?"

Some cops needed to be charmed, others needed to be challenged. Prince could read Haller in thirty seconds. Small-town authority used to deference, probably counting days until retirement. The type who'd rather preserve departmental dignity than solve cases.

The message landed hard. Haller bristled, clearly offended, but cleared his throat.

"Absolutely," he said, tightening. "That would be good."

"Is there a controlled environment where we can review your evidence? A conference room, perhaps?"

Haller stood. "Follow me."

The conference room smelled like dust and stale coffee. Prince and Wilbur, now sleeved up, hunched over glossy crime scene photos, flipping through autopsy reports and witness statements with practiced precision. Haller stood by the wall, arms crossed, like a man who didn't belong in the room anymore.

"She was a student, no?" Prince asked, eyes down.

"College student," Haller said. "Freshman at UVA. Last year's valedictorian. Just home for the holidays."

Wilbur shuffled to a graduation photo. He held it up.

"Gorgeous girl," Haller said, solemn. He shook his head.

"Sheriff, do you have any of Evelyn's personal belongings?" Prince asked. "Laptop, perhaps?"

"We haven't searched the home."

Prince paused. "What?"

"They're grieving," Haller said, bristling.

"Have you spoken to the father?"

"Last time was when I broke the news. He's gone off the rails. Drinking, shouting at press—"

"I need to speak to the father," Prince said. He stood and grabbed his jacket. Wilbur followed.

"He's a difficult man," Haller offered.

"And we're law enforcement," Prince shot back, throwing the jacket on. "Try it sometime."

Haller's neck flushed red at the shot. *Who the fuck does this—*

"There's something you won't find in that report," he said, a last-ditch swing for control.

Prince froze, turned. "Excuse me?"

"She was eleven weeks pregnant."

"And why wasn't that in the report?"

"I had it omitted."

Prince's cheeks flushed. "You did what?"

"I had it taken out—"

"I know what the fuck 'omitted' means. Why would you do that?"

"I didn't want the father to find out."

"You mean a potential suspect?"

"The victim's father, goddammit," Haller snapped. "Richard. The guy's a fucking head case. I feared it might put him over the edge. He's already on the precipice."

"You doctored evidence—"

"Drop it!" Haller barked. "You know now. That's what matters. I'm clean—cleaner than most—but I wasn't going to let him find out that way. Not through some goddamn M.E. report. You want to file a complaint, take my badge? Be my guest!"

"Yeah," Prince said, voice rising, "I just might!"

Haller waved him off. Awkwardly, clumsily. Like an old man trying to pick a fight he knew he'd lose. He turned, paced toward the other end of the room, gripping his belt like it could hold his pride together.

Prince cracked the door for Wilbur, then looked back and locked eyes with Haller one last time.

"Thin ice, Sheriff," he said through a tight jaw.

"Thin fuckin' ice."

The media frenzy outside the Armstrongs had dwindled. Now just a CNN van, a FOX Escalade, and a battered van from TMZ New York remained, idling like vultures in the cold.

Prince remembered the first time he drove up to the

Armstrong home. It looked haunted. Shrouded in a passing mist, a skeletal maple tree looming over the sagging roof like a sentinel left behind by better seasons. Winter had already taken its first bite. The street looked like the aftermath of a failed ambush. Big Gulp cups, cigarette butts, Taco Bell wrappers scattered like shell casings. *Skeletons of the spineless*, Prince thought.

He parked at the foot of the steep driveway. He and Wilbur exited in unison, badges dangling from their necks, drawing murmurs from the few third-rate journalists still lurking with red-rimmed eyes.

Prince reached the front door and knocked three times.

"Mr. Armstrong, this is Special Agent James Prince with partner Christopher Wilbur from the FBI. May we have a word?"

Nothing.

Prince knocked again. "Mr. Armstrong, are you home?"

Something shattered inside.

"Fuck!" a man boomed.

"Mr. Armstrong? Is that you? Are you okay?"

Footsteps followed. Light, wary. Then came the slow creak of floorboards under idle weight.

"Special who?"

"Special Agent James Prince, sir. New York FBI."

A pause.

"Ah," the man breathed, unimpressed. "What do you need?"

"To speak with you, sir. If you wouldn't mind."

Another beat of silence. Then the lock began to turn. Wilbur glanced over his shoulder; a few reporters were starting to raise their cameras.

The door opened.

It was Richard Armstrong.

He wasn't shaving, that much was clear. Possibly not bathing either. But it was his eyes that struck Prince. They weren't just glazed. They were void. Not clouded. Not tired. Empty. Each glance reeked of whiskey and despair. Prince saw it immediately: a heart beyond repair. A darkness that didn't blink.

Prince recognized the look immediately. The thousand-yard stare of someone who'd witnessed too much horror, absorbed too much loss. He'd seen it in combat veterans, in parents of murdered children, in mirrors after particularly brutal cases. Richard Armstrong was walking wounded, held together by whiskey and rage.

The smell hit first as they were ushered inside. Stale liquor, sweat, old grief. The house was a shrine to what had been: family photos on every wall, Evelyn's awards and certificates displayed proudly, a coat still hanging by the door like she might come claim it.

Richard led them to the living room. Empty bottles surrounded an overstuffed chair like fallen soldiers. He collapsed into it, reaching for a half-empty fifth of Jim Beam.

"Mr. Armstrong, have you issued a statement since the discovery of the body?" Prince asked.

"No."

Prince set a recorder on the coffee table. "Would it be alright if this served as such?"

Richard nodded. Prince hit record.

"Can you think of anyone who would've wanted to do this to your daughter?"

"Who the fuck would want to do that to anybody?" Richard rasped. He poured another serving, took a sip. "No. I can't."

The agents sat in matching chairs across from him.

Richard slumped on the sofa, barefoot in a tattered gray bathrobe. He smelled of cigarettes. His lips were red and shiny from the whiskey. His hair was oily and uncombed.

"How's Janet?" Prince asked. "Your wife."

"Doesn't leave the bed much."

"And you?"

Richard forced a smile. Crooked, yellow, and awful. He'd have been better off not trying. "I manage."

Prince nodded like he believed it and moved on. Functional alcoholics were Prince's specialty. He'd been one himself, knew the rhythm of maintenance drinking, the careful calibration between numb and coherent. Richard was past that point. Drowning instead of floating. Which made him either useless as a witness or dangerous as a suspect. "It's our understanding Evelyn went to a party the night of her disappearance with a Sarah Willoughby. Were you aware of anyone they were hoping to meet?"

"It was at that boy's house. Dylan Smith. Great ball player. Parents have money."

"Was Evelyn close with him?"

"No. That kind of stuff was more Sarah's scene. Evelyn liked her books. Liked her home."

"Any people in her life we should know about?" Prince asked. "Ex-boyfriends?"

"She was seeing one boy," Richard said. "Frankie Lopez. No-good kid from a no-good family. Lives in the trailer park. Works at the mill with his dad."

Prince scribbled the name.

"Never understood it," Richard muttered.

Prince looked up. "Understood what?"

"The union."

"You didn't think he was good enough."

"Not by a mile."

Prince regarded the bottle between Richard's knees with a squint. "You a heavy drinker, Mr. Armstrong?"

"Relevance?"

"In your statement to Sheriff Haller, you mentioned imbibing an unknown amount the night Evelyn went missing."

"I like to drink and jam out a little when I write."

"Yeah? What were you working on?"

"Piece for the local paper. Parade coverage."

"You get it out?"

Richard grunted. "Didn't make it this year."

Prince and Wilbur exchanged a look. Wilbur picked it up from there.

"Mr. Armstrong, we'd like to sweep your daughter's room. Our understanding is no formal inventory was ever conducted."

"Yeah," Richard said, detached. "That's fine."

"This is what we do," Prince told him. "We will find who did this."

Richard blinked, then gave a half-smile. This one was real. Weightless, almost. And in that moment, Prince felt something sharp twist in his gut. A prod of doubt. A question he hadn't yet formed. There was something in Richard's expression that didn't belong. A flicker of satisfaction, maybe even anticipation. Prince had learned to trust these moments, when his subconscious picked up signals his rational mind hadn't processed yet.

"Better get on it."

They climbed the stairs to Evelyn's bedroom. A museum of a life interrupted. A corkboard filled with college acceptance letters. Volleyball trophies. A neat stack of true crime novels beside the bed. Wilbur moved to the desk. Prince lingered in the doorway, struck by the stillness in the air.

"Let's start with her laptop," Prince said, pointing to the MacBook. "Comms. Search history. Then we'll coordinate with Haller to bring in the ex-boyfriend."

Wilbur booted it up. Prince moved to the bulletin board, scanning photos of Evelyn and her friends. In several, a scowling, dark-haired boy hovered close to her. Presumably Frankie Lopez. He never smiled. But his arm was always around her.

"Hey, look at this," Wilbur called, nodding at the screen. "Last searches before she came home: 'early pregnancy symptoms,' 'abortion options New York State,' 'how to tell boyfriend about abortion.'"

The pregnancy changed everything. Suddenly this wasn't just about a college girl who trusted the wrong person. It was about secrets, shame, and the kind of desperation that turned ordinary people into killers.

"Definitely wasn't shopping for cribs," Wilbur muttered.

Over the next twenty-four hours, the laptop was scrubbed. Evelyn had searched for abortion providers, in-network urgent care, and not much else. It was noted.

Her ex-roommate, Madison, didn't expect a call from the FBI mid-lecture. She stepped into a UVA stairwell and spoke to Prince for thirteen minutes. Yes, she knew about the pregnancy. Yes, they'd argued over it.

It was noted.

Prince and Wilbur spoke to Dylan Smith and several partygoers. All said the same: Frankie had been unusually fixated on Evelyn that night.

It was noted.

By Wednesday evening, Prince stood before a wall in the sheriff's conference room, now covered with photographs, statements, and sticky notes forming a constellation that still didn't quite connect.

It was still snowing when Prince pulled up to the Armstrong house again. The porch light buzzed above the entryway, its glow barely cutting through the falling white. He wasn't here officially. No warrant. Just a gut feeling and a bad taste in his mouth.

Janet answered the door after the second knock. Her hair was damp, tied back carelessly, and she wore a thick cardigan over a faded T-shirt. No makeup. Just tired eyes.

"Mr. Prince," she said, trying for composure. "It's late."

"I know. I just... I had a few questions I didn't get to earlier. About Evelyn."

She hesitated, then opened the door wider. "Come in. But be quiet. Richard's asleep out back."

Prince stepped inside. The place smelled like pine cleaner and burnt coffee. A photo of Evelyn sat crooked on the mantle.

They talked in the living room. Quiet voices. Just small things at first. Evelyn's moods, her grades, her relationship with Frankie. Janet answered them all like someone reading from an old diary. Detached. Careful.

Then her hand trembled when she set down her tea.

"She was good," Janet said softly. "Too good. I think that's what did it. Goodness makes people angry. You notice that?"

Prince watched her. "I've noticed."

She looked at him, really looked. Something in her face cracking open.

"Richard hasn't touched me in almost a year," she said suddenly. "Not like a husband should."

She laughed, but there was nothing funny in it. "Hell, he barely speaks to me unless it's about Evelyn or the damn dog. Sometimes I think I don't even live here. I'm just haunting it."

Prince hesitated, then stood. Moved to her gently. "Janet—"

"I'm sorry," she said, wiping her eyes quickly. "I don't mean to—"

He stepped closer. Instinctively. Carefully. And then, just for a moment, he hugged her. One hand on her back, the other resting awkwardly on her shoulder. She melted into it like a woman starved. Clung tighter than he expected. Her breath caught in her throat. Prince recognized the hunger in her touch. The need for human contact that had nothing to do with attraction and everything to do with survival.

They separated slowly. Prince looked away first.

"I should go," he said.

She nodded, stepping back, tucking hair behind her ear. "Thank you, detective."

He didn't say anything else. Just let the door close softly behind him, the snow already burying his footsteps.

The picture was fragmented.

But one name kept surfacing.

CHAPTER TWELVE

INTERROGATION

DECEMBER 1, 2022

The agents had picked Frankie up at 8:08 A.M. for "minor" questioning and transported him to the Bronxville Sheriff's Department. He'd thrown on a white wife beater in haste, sweatpants sagging, hair messy, eyes wide. He sat clumsily in the "interrogation room," which was really just a stuffy conference room with four beige walls and a circular mahogany table gifted by the church years back. Wrists free, he waited thirty minutes with nothing but burnt Folgers in styrofoam and the groan of the air vent. Only when his head began to dip—

Bang. Prince and a folder-bearing Wilbur entered the room. Prince took to the corner silently. Wilbur slid into the seat across from Frankie and split the folder open.

"Good morning, Mr. Lopez. I'm Special Agent

Christopher Wilbur. Beside me is Special Agent James Prince."

Frankie rubbed his eyes. "The fuck am I doing here?"

Wilbur offered a dry smile. "I ask myself the same thing whenever I'm in a town like this and remember I passed the bar with a 280 just to choose the Bureau. Could've had a window office and a pension by now."

He opened the folder. "Instead, I get to hang out with you. So let's make it worth it. What was your relationship with Evelyn Armstrong?"

"We were friends."

"Friends?"

"Good friends."

"Boyfriend and girlfriend?"

"At times."

"At times?"

"Yeah, that's right."

Wilbur raised an eyebrow. "How about all the time?"

"I'm saying it didn't always feel like it. We led different lives."

"As in?"

"You need me to spell it out?"

"The valedictorian and the jailbird, huh?"

Frankie smiled, tired. "I know my place in life, sir."

"What time did you leave the party?"

"What party?"

"Dylan Smith's. November 19th."

"I don't know. 10:30?"

"Is that a guess?"

"I left after Evelyn did."

From the corner, Prince studied him. Despite the tough-guy act, he saw fear—tight shoulders, twitchy hands, flicking eyes. The question was whether it came from guilt… or just being nineteen and in deep shit.

"Where did you go?" Wilbur asked.

"The park. Kept drinking."

"Can anyone corroborate that?"

"Corroborate solo drinking?"

"No, then." Wilbur scribbled something. "Mr. Lopez, were you aware Ms. Armstrong was with child?"

Frankie flinched. Wilbur's pen paused.

"You were aware?"

"Yeah."

"How'd you find out?"

"She called me from school."

"How'd you feel about it?"

"I thought it was exciting. She didn't."

"You're saying she wasn't pleased."

"No, I'm saying she *freaked*. Got fuckin' crazy."

"Were you aware she was seeking an abortion?"

"Pretty clear she was."

"You figured, or you knew?"

"She said she wasn't keeping it. So *yeah*, I guess I knew! Jesus, what the fuck are you asking me?"

"You understand how this looks, right?"

"Excuse me?"

"You don't even realize how bad this has gone."

"Wilbur," Prince cut in.

Wilbur cleared his throat, stood, and walked to the door.

"Francisco Lopez, you're being placed under arrest on suspicion of the murder of Evelyn Armstrong."

"The fuck—"

Wilbur knocked twice. Nichols and Brownlee entered. Brownlee yanked Frankie up and cuffed him while Nichols hovered nearby. Frankie thrashed, cursing, as Wilbur read his rights.

"Wait, you think I *did* this shit?!"

Prince slipped out into the hallway.

He leaned against the wall, thinking. Frankie's reaction hadn't been calculated—it was rage, confusion, raw fear. But it didn't clear him. Prince had seen killers put on better shows. What bothered him was the timing. If the pregnancy sparked a confrontation... why wait until she was home? Why not confront her at school, where there were fewer eyes?

Boots echoed down the hall.

"You get your man?" Sheriff Haller asked. Casual voice. Cold eyes.

"Person of interest," Prince said. "Strong motive. Weak alibi."

"You talk to Richard?"

"Something like that."

"Bet that was pleasant."

Prince didn't respond.

"He say anything useful?"

"He said a lot. None of it helpful."

Haller exhaled. "You look him up?"

"No."

"You should look him up."

Prince raised an eyebrow. Haller was already walking away.

Back in the car, Prince opened his Bureau tablet and typed *Richard James Armstrong*. It took a moment—classified filters, clearance pings, an authorization gate he hadn't seen since digging into Cold War files for fun.

Then the file loaded.

NAME: ARMSTRONG, RICHARD J.

UNIT: ST3 DEVGRU – Naval Special Warfare Development Group

STATUS: Retired – Honorable Discharge

CLEARANCE LEVEL: Tier 1 – Red Flag Classification

RANK: Chief Petty Officer (CPO), U.S. Navy SEAL

SPECIALTY

– Close Quarters Combat (CQC)

– Enhanced Interrogation Techniques

– Asymmetrical Response Operations (Domestic & Foreign)

– High-Risk Extraction & Recon

– Psychological Pressure Protocols

TOUR RECORD

– Classified (Operations in Kandahar, Ramadi, Mali, undisclosed Eastern European targets)

– Joint Task Force Ops with CIA SAD-SOG

– Honor Citation for Operation Glass Storm (file sealed)

POST-SERVICE NOTES

– Transferred to DOJ for field profiling; declined full-time

– Subject exhibits signs of unresolved trauma and operational fatigue

– Considered unstable, but not dangerous, unless reactivated or provoked

Prince stared at the screen, pulse slowing.

He hadn't just worn a badge. He *was* the badge—the kind they send in when missions go off-book and nobody's supposed to come back.

Richard had belonged to the most elite SEAL unit on the planet. Trusted to start wars—and finish them. Alone.

And now he was drunk. Broken.

Sitting at the center of a murder investigation.

Frankie's $5,000 bail was cashed the next morning at 9:18 A.M. from a Bank of America branch in Yonkers by Roger Lopez, and Frankie was thereby released.

"What's going on, Frank?"

"I don't know, Pop," Frankie said. "Wasn't me did this, I promise."

"Hell, I know that."

Frankie looked at his father. "How'd you come up with the money?"

"Don't you worry —"

"How?" Frankie pressed.

There was a hard silence. "Savings, mostly."

"Should've just left me, Pop," Frankie said, shaking his head emphatically. "I've been worse off."

"Nonsense," Roger said, "Don't you worry," and it was then that the old man began to cry.

Roger and Frankie sat at their small kitchen table later, the weight of everything that had happened pressing down on them. The trailer creaked and groaned around them, the wind finding its way through poorly sealed windows.

"They think I killed her," Frankie said, his voice hollow. "They think I could do that to Evelyn."

"They're looking for someone easy to blame," Roger replied, wiping his eyes with a weathered hand. "You've got a record. You're from the trailer park. To them, we're already guilty."

"I loved her, Pop," Frankie whispered, tears welling in his eyes. "I know I said some terrible things when she told me about the... about the baby. But I would never hurt her.

Never. I loved her *so* much, Pop..."

Roger placed a hand on his son's shoulder. "I know that, son. And that's why we're going to fight this."

The television flickered in the corner like it was trying to keep a secret. Local news. Volume turned down low, like someone didn't want to hear the truth too clearly. Onscreen, a reporter stood stiff as a corpse outside the Bronxville Sheriff's Department, lips moving like she was casting a spell. Behind her, Evelyn Armstrongs photo lingered—smiling, bright-eyed, still alive in that way only the dead can be.

"What do we do now?" Frankie asked, voice brittle.

Roger's expression hardened. "We lay low. And we watch our backs."

"You think they'll come for me again?"

Roger didn't answer immediately. Didn't blink either. His eyes were locked on the screen, where Evelyn vanished and was replaced by a grainy photo of Richard Armstrong in full Navy get-up. Caption: *Father of the Deceased*. He was younger in the photo, though no less severe—expressionless, unreadable, like he was already staring down their graves.

Roger's jaw tightened.

"I think," the old man said carefully, "that there may be more dangerous things in this town right now than the police."

Outside, the first flakes of snow began to fall, a harbinger of the storm to come.

MURDER IN BRONXVILLE

BY JONATHAN EVANS

THE IDYLLIC VILLAGE of Bronxville, New York—a picture-perfect enclave of historic homes nestled among oaks and maples—is on edge following the discovery of a beloved daughter's body in what residents are calling the most shocking crime in memory.

Evelyn Armstrong, 18, whose academic brilliance and warm spirit had made her a standout even in this affluent community, was found dead in Twin Lakes County Park, transforming a cherished local sanctuary into a scene of horror.

"It feels like the heart has been ripped out of our village," said Eleanor Whitman, 63, who once taught Armstrong piano. "Evelyn wasn't just another bright student—she was special. The kind of young person who made you believe in the future."

Armstrong, who had delivered a stirring valedictorian address just months earlier at Bronxville High, had returned home from her freshman year at the University of Virginia to celebrate Thanksgiving with her family. It ended in tragedy on what should have been a night of reunion.

The events began at a gathering on Masterson Road, where Armstrong left with longtime friend Sarah Willoughby. "She just wanted to get out," Willoughby told police. "I begged her to get back in the car. It was so cold, and it was dark... I should have tried harder."

Authorities quickly detained Armstrong's former boyfriend, Francisco "Frankie" Lopez, but released him on $5,000 bail, sparking outrage. "How do you put a price tag on a girl's life?" asked Margaret Stevens, 47, a neighbor. "This isn't justice. It's an insult."

Lopez, through his attorney, maintained his innocence, calling Armstrong's death "a devastating loss" and vowing cooperation.

For Richard and Janet Armstrong, accomplished professionals who had built their lives around their only child's future, the nightmare continues behind drawn curtains in their Dutch Colonial on Lookout Avenue. The home sits silent, now fronted by flowers, candles, and notes while news vans linger nearby.

"I haven't seen either of them," whispered neighbor Martha Miles, 78. "The lights go on and off, so we know they're in there, but... how do you even begin to live through something like this?"

FBI agents have now joined local law enforcement, collecting surveillance footage and conducting interviews across Westchester. Sources suggest evidence may conflict with early theories, though officials declined to comment.

Bronxville High has postponed its winter formal and created a memorial scholarship in Armstrong's name. Blue and gold ribbons, once tied to her academic triumphs, now mark a life cut short.

"She was going to change the world," said William Baker, her former biology teacher, speaking at a candlelight vigil. "Some students pass through your classroom, but others leave an indelible mark. Evelyn was luminous—brilliant in every sense."

As winter descends on Bronxville, residents are left asking uncomfortable questions about safety, justice, and the fragility of life in a place where tragedy was something that happened elsewhere—until now.

The Armstrong family has requested privacy at this time.

CHAPTER THIRTEEN

THE PHOTOGRAPH

DECEMBER 5, 2022

Blue light crept through the thin curtains of the inn like a reluctant intruder, pale and cold. Prince woke to the sound of nothing. That kind of stillness only found in small towns where the world hadn't yet stirred.

The bedside clock read 6:16 A.M., the thermostat 59°. He stared up at the ceiling. It was cracked and the plaster was beginning to peel in long, curling strips. The radiator clanked somewhere in the corner, struggling to warm the room. It smelled a bit of mildew and old wood, and the scent seemed to cling to the worn-out floral wallpaper that had seen better decades. Or centuries.

Prince finally sat up, joints stiff from the cheap mattress.

Goddamn thing sags in the middle.

A dull ache throbbed at the base of his skull, rudely

reminding him of the pint of Chivas he'd impulsively purchased at the Local Mart before turning in.

He rubbed a hand over his jaw, feeling stubble, and let out a sigh, eliciting a geyser of visible breath. He then swung his arm over to the nightstand and scraped a crumpled pack of Marlboro Lights off the smooth surface. He plucked one out and lit it in bed.

Three days and eight hours had passed since the release of Frankie Lopez and Prince felt just the same as he did upon arresting the boy.

Nothing at all.

Not to say he believed he was innocent. In fact, since they'd touched down in the village, Prince might argue that no one had proven to be truly innocent in the greater sense of the designation.

Sheriff Haller? Concealed evidence. General putz.

Richard Armstrong? A resentful, crude, absent-minded drunk.

And Frankie? Certainly not a runner-up for Boyfriend of the Year.

But a killer?

Unlikely. Too emotional. He'd fight the wind if he could.

Prince grunted and swung his legs over, cigarette hanging out of his mouth. He walked over to the door and opened it, letting in a brisk flood of air which promptly hardened his nipples. He leaned up against the doorway and took a drag, fixating on the dense woods across the way.

Who are you?

It began to rain.

The case was stalling, and Prince knew it. After the initial flurry of activity. The arrest and release of Frankie Lopez, the revelation about Evelyn's pregnancy. They had hit a wall. No new leads, no unexpected witnesses coming forward, no physical evidence beyond what they'd already collected.

Just a dead girl, a grieving family, and a town closing ranks against outsiders.

"So what's the gaff?" Wilbur said, setting his palms up in a booth at Maryanne's Cafe. Rain pattered against the window. "Kid knocks her up and she doesn't want it. Fair enough. Why kill her that way?"

"The curtains," Prince muttered, chewing his eggs. "One's lower than the other."

"What?"

"Nothing."

"What the fuck are you on about?"

"I don't like the Lopez kid for it."

"And?"

A shrug. "I don't like it."

"Well, what *do* you like?" Wilbur countered facetiously, just as Prince clocked the man in a cream-colored windbreaker and black aviators flashing photos of their sedan outside.

"Not that," Prince said, and flew from the booth and out into the wet street, shoving the photographer a few paces back.

"Who the fuck are you and what are you doing?" Prince snarled.

"Woah, woah, woah!" the man bawled, tucking the Canon and outstretching a bony hand, fingertips stained with yellow highlighter. "Jonathan Evans, *New York Times*."

"And?"

"Well, usually, this is the part where you tell me what your name is."

"What do you want?"

"You're here on account of the Armstrong girl, aren't you?"

"None of your business—"

"I'm putting together a story," Evans went on. "I think it could be big."

Prince just stared at him. Evans reached into his pocket and unsheathed a business card.

"Maybe we can help each other," Evans said. "I might know more than you think."

"Like what?"

"James!"

Evans' smile didn't waver. "Like who's doing it."

"James!"

Prince turned. Wilbur stuck out of the diner's entrance like an inflatable man, waving his phone.

"Package at the department. Addressed to you."

Prince gave a nod, turned back.

Evans was already gone.

The envelope was plain, almost insultingly so. It bore no postage, no return address. Just *Special Agent James Prince and co.* written in neat cursive across the front.

It sat in the center of Haller's desk like a coiled snake, its plain surface mocking the tension in the room. Prince stood over it, arms crossed and jaw tight.

"Showed up an hour ago," Haller said. "No postage. No prints on the envelope. Just your name."

Wilbur was leaning against the doorframe, eyes narrowing. "Fuck's in it?"

Prince snatched it off the desk and tore it open with his fingernails. Slowly, he began to push a thin, rectangular item out from the envelope with his thumbs, until...

A Polaroid photograph plopped onto the desk, unfurling to reveal seemingly a lewd portrait of a young girl with black hair in red lingerie, posed on a divan with a lit cigarette propped between her thin fingers like it belonged there. In the bottom left corner, labeled crudely in bold Sharpie, was *18th BIRTHDAY.* Prince promptly unclasped his briefcase and pulled out a pair of blue latex gloves from a lower compartment, which was then followed by tweezers and a sample evidence bag which he lay neatly beside Haller's desk lamp.

He plucked the right top corner of the Polaroid and held it up to his view. Wilbur was there now, peering over Prince's shoulder.

It was Evelyn.

"That your girl, Sheriff?" Prince said, holding it for display. Haller's brow formed a doughy V. Prince sucked his teeth, bagged it, and looked to Wilbur:

"Run it down to the white coats," he said, handing him the evidence bag. "I want prints dusted by lunch."

It was 2:10 P.M. at Bronxville High.

The gymnasium echoed with sneaker squeaks and adolescent laughter as a class of thirty co-eds prepared for indoor dodgeball. Rain lashed against the high windows, painting watery shadows across the polished floor. Van Reynolds stood at center court, whistle hanging from his neck like a silver pendulum, his stance casual but commanding.

Van was the kind of athletic director who made an impression. Early thirties with the build of someone who hadn't let go of his glory days, hair meticulously styled into a faux hawk that wouldn't dare move even during wind sprints. His square-framed glasses housed eyes of deceptive warmth. Earthy green irises that suggested kindness, approachability, a man comfortable in his own skin. The kids trusted those eyes. The parents did too. That was his gift.

"Van Reynolds!"

The name cracked through the gymnasium like a gunshot. Thirty teenage heads swiveled in unison. The oxygen seemed to evacuate the room in one collective gasp as dodgeballs rolled forgotten across the court.

Sheriff Joseph Haller stood at the double doors, flanked by Deputies Brownlee and Nichols. Their black-and-yellow windbreakers. Stark against the school's red and white color scheme. Might as well have been hazmat suits for the way they announced trouble. Their badges caught the fluorescent lights, flashing like warning beacons.

Van's professional smile faltered, then reassembled itself. "Can I help you gentlemen?"

"We need you to come with us," Haller said, voice flat as a closed book.

"Is something wrong?"

"Mr. Reynolds," Haller's tone lowered, "it would be in your best interest to mirror our discretion until we're off campus."

Something electric and terrible passed behind Van's eyes. A muscle in his left eyelid began to twitch. A nervous tell he thought he'd buried with his teenage insecurities. He turned to his students, whose faces had transformed from exertion-flushed to anxious in seconds.

"Keep playing, guys," he managed, voice steady despite the crimson creeping up his neck. "A staff member will be in shortly."

The squeak of the deputies' boots against the polished floor seemed unnaturally loud as they escorted Van from the gym. Each step echoed with finality. The sound of a life about to unravel, thread by careful thread.

The interrogation room at the Bronxville Sheriff's Department was a study in institutional indifference. Beige walls, fluorescent lights that hummed like angry wasps, and a metal table bolted to the floor. The air smelled of coffee gone cold and fear-sweat soaked into decades of bad decisions.

Van Reynolds sat with his hands flat on the table, fingers splayed like pale starfish. His perfectly styled faux hawk had begun to wilt, a few strands falling across his forehead. He'd been waiting for forty-three minutes. A deliberate tactic that Prince had insisted upon. Let him stew. Let the silence work on him.

When the door finally opened, Reynolds straightened, composing his features into what he clearly hoped was innocent concern. Special Agent Wilbur entered first, manila folder tucked under his arm, followed by Sheriff Haller, who positioned himself against the wall. Prince slipped in last, choosing to remain in the shadows by the one-way glass, watching.

"Mr. Reynolds, I'm Special Agent Christopher Wilbur with the FBI," Wilbur began, settling into the metal chair across from Van. The legs screeched against the linoleum. A discordant note that made Van flinch. "I appreciate your cooperation."

"Of course," Van replied, voice steady despite the film of sweat on his upper lip. "Anything to help. Although I'm still not clear why I was brought in like this. In front of my students."

Wilbur ignored the implicit complaint, opening his folder with methodical precision. "Mr. Reynolds, what was the nature of your relationship with Ms. Armstrong?"

"She was a student of mine," Van replied, the words hollow and rehearsed.

Prince studied the man's body language from his position in the corner. Reynolds had good control. Better than most. But the tells were there: the slight elevation in his breathing, the way his right foot had begun to tap silently against the floor.

Wilbur consulted his notes with theatrical care. "I understand you've served as AD and varsity volleyball coach for the local high school since... 2016. Correct?"

"Correct." The word hung in the air, lonely.

"When did you meet Ms. Armstrong, Mr. Reynolds?"

"I'd have to say around 2018."

"2018. So that puts her as, what, a freshman?"

"Yes, sir." Van's fingers drummed a nervous rhythm on the metal table, then stilled as he caught himself.

Wilbur nodded, marking something in his notes. "Would you say you knew her well?"

"As well as any teacher knows their students, I suppose." Van shifted in his seat. "She was on the volleyball team her freshman and sophomore years. Talented, but not exceptional. She quit junior year to focus on academics."

"Hmm." Wilbur made another note. "Did you have much contact with her after she left the team?"

Van hesitated. A microsecond pause that screamed in the quiet room. "Not particularly. I'd see her in the halls, of course. Small school."

Prince pushed off from the wall and paced slowly behind Wilbur. He could see the effect his movement had on Reynolds. The teacher's eyes tracking him like prey watching a predator.

"Let's talk about your whereabouts on Saturday, November 19th," Wilbur continued. "The night Evelyn Armstrong disappeared."

"I was home." Van's voice remained steady. "Grading some Geography papers, watching TV. Nothing exciting."

"Can anyone confirm that?"

"I live alone."

"No visitors? No phone calls? No pizza delivery?" Wilbur's tone was casual, but the questions were pointed darts.

Van shook his head. "I'm a creature of habit, Agent Wilbur. Saturday nights are usually pretty quiet for me."

"What were you watching?" Prince interjected suddenly.

Van blinked, turning slightly to face him. "Excuse me?"

"On TV. What were you watching?"

"Oh. Um, a Celtics game, I think. They were playing the Knicks."

Prince smiled thinly. "Interesting. The Celtics played the Hawks that night. The Knicks game was Friday."

A flush crept up Van's neck. "Then it was the Hawks. I don't really follow basketball that closely. I just had it on as background."

"Background for what?" Prince pressed.

"For grading, like I said."

Wilbur cleared his throat, reclaiming control of the interrogation. "And when exactly did you begin your sexual relationship with Ms. Armstrong?"

The question landed like a blow. Van's face drained of color. "Excuse me?"

Wilbur produced a sealed evidence bag containing a Polaroid and slid it across the scratched metal surface. "We received this image via express mail earlier today. Prints on the film led back to you."

Van stared at the photograph, his mouth working silently before finding words. "What the fuck is this?" He slumped backward as though the chair were suddenly his only anchor in a tilting world.

"Mr. Reynolds, you're going to want to be very careful with how you answer what I'm about to ask you," Wilbur said, his calm more threatening than any raised voice. "Did you take this photograph?"

Van's composure finally shattered completely. "I think I'd like a lawyer."

Prince unfolded from the shadows, his movement sudden as a striking snake. "Fuck you," he snarled. "Answer the question."

Van's eyes flickered between the two agents, a trapped animal calculating escape routes where none existed. "I did *not* send this in—"

"That's not what he asked you." Prince's voice was winter in August.

Haller stirred uncomfortably against the wall, but said nothing. This was federal territory now.

Van began to scratch at his hands, raw patches forming under his fingernails. "I didn't mean for it."

"Didn't mean for what, exactly?" Wilbur pressed, pen poised like a weapon.

"She was such a smart girl," Van said, voice softening to something like reverence. "Just... beyond her years. I didn't mean to. I never..."

"You never what?" Prince leaned in, invading Van's space.

"I never meant for it to go as far as it did." His voice cracked like thin ice. "She... I started doing one-on-ones with her. To work on her serve."

"When was that?" Wilbur asked, pen clicking. The sound of tiny bones breaking.

"That was when she was around sixteen," Van admitted, eyes downcast. "It progressed to coffees. Then it was episodes of *Supernatural* at my condo. It was all very harmless for a while. I made sure of it."

"'Harmless,'" Prince repeated, the word twisted with contempt. "Is that what you tell yourself?"

Van's face contorted, a glimpse of genuine emotion breaking through. "She was mature. She understood—"

"She was a child. And you were her teacher."

"At what point did it become intimate?" Wilbur redirected, maintaining the rhythm of the interrogation.

Van swallowed hard. "The day after her eighteenth

birthday."

"How convenient," Prince murmured.

"Yeah. Yeah, I took the fucking picture," Van confessed, words spilling out now. "But I-I'd lost it. I swear to God, I didn't mark it or send it in, I wouldn't—"

"When did you last see it?" Wilbur interrupted.

Van blinked, momentarily thrown. "The photo? I don't know. Maybe six months ago? I kept it in a box in my closet with... other things."

"Other trophies?" Prince reentered.

"No! Just... letters, gifts. Mementos."

"From other students?" Prince's voice was dangerously soft.

"No. Only Evelyn." Van's eyes darted to Haller, then back to Wilbur, seeking a more sympathetic face. "Look, I know how this looks. I made a mistake. A serious lapse in judgment. But I cared about her."

"Did you care about her on the night of November 19th?" Wilbur asked.

The question hung in the air. Van's face went slack.

"What?"

"Where really were you that night, Van?" Prince moved closer, looming over the seated man. "Because we have a witness who places your car near Twin Lakes Park around midnight. That's not far from where Evelyn's body was found."

It was a lie. A calculated shot in the dark. But the effect on Van was immediate. His breathing quickened, pupils dilating.

"That's not possible," he stammered. "I was home all night. I didn't go anywhere near Twin Lakes."

"So our witness is lying?" Wilbur asked.

"Yes! I mean... there must be some mistake. Maybe

someone else has a similar car. I drive a gray Camry. There are thousands of them."

Prince pulled out a chair and sat directly across from Van, their faces now level. "Here's what I think happened, Van. I think Evelyn was breaking it off. Moving on. College girl now, whole life ahead of her. And you couldn't handle that, could you?"

"No, that's not—"

"She told you it was over, and something in you snapped. The same thing that snapped when you first decided a sixteen-year-old girl was 'fair game.' The little voice that whispers you deserve whatever you want."

"I didn't hurt her," Van insisted, the first tears welling in his eyes. "I loved her."

"When was the last time you saw her?" Wilbur asked.

Van wiped at his eyes with the back of his hand. "October. Before she left for college. We met at Starbucks in White Plains. She... she did end things. Said she wanted a clean slate at UVA. But it was amicable. I understood."

"And you never contacted her after that?" Prince's skepticism was palpable.

"We texted a few times. Nothing serious."

"Show us," Wilbur said.

"What?"

"Your phone," Prince echoed, overenunciating the way one might to a child. "Show us the texts."

Van hesitated. "I deleted them. After... after I heard what happened to her. I panicked. I knew how it would look."

"Exactly like what it is?"

"No! I was scared, that's all. I knew people would assume—"

"That you killed her?" Prince finished. "Why would

they assume that, Van, unless there was a reason to?"

"Because of our relationship! Because I'm the older man, the authority figure. I'm always going to be the villain in that story."

Prince leaned back, studying the athletic director with cold calculation. "Did you take trophies from your other victims too?"

"Victims? What other victims?" Genuine confusion crossed Van's face. "There's only ever been Evelyn."

"What about Miley McDermott?" Wilbur asked, sliding another photo across the table. This one a missing persons flyer. "Seventeen. Disappeared from Scarsdale last month. Never found."

Van looked genuinely baffled. "I've never seen this girl in my life."

"Are you sure? Her billboards are everywhere."

"I had nothing to do with this," Van insisted, his voice cracking. "Nothing."

Prince studied him intently. Either Van Reynolds was the most accomplished liar he'd ever encountered, or the man was telling the truth. At least about the McDermott girl.

"And where were you on the night of November 19th, 2022?" Wilbur asked again, circling back.

"I... Watching TV, I think? That was a Saturday, right?"

"Can that be corroborated?"

Van shrugged helplessly. "I live alone, detective."

Wilbur closed his binder with a snap of finality. He exchanged a glance with Prince, who decided it was his turn.

"Mr. Reynolds, you're being placed under arrest on suspicion for the murder of Evelyn Armstrong," Prince announced, standing. "You have the right to an attorney.

Anything you say can and will be used against you in a court of law—"

"I'm sorry, murder?" The word seemed to physically strike Van, his body jolting backward.

"You have the right to an attorney. If you cannot afford an attorney, one will be provided for you—"

"Would you just stop, please?" Van's voice rose, panic overtaking any attempt at composure.

Prince continued the Miranda litany, implacable as a funeral director. "If you decide to answer questions now without an attorney present, you will still have the right to stop answering at any time you speak to an attorney..."

"This is fucking bullshit, I can't..." Van's breathing accelerated, his chest heaving beneath his polo shirt.

Again, Deputy Brownlee entered, handcuffs dangling from his thick fingers like chrome jewelry.

"I-I didn't kill Evelyn," Van stammered, desperation turning to pleading. "I was irresponsible, yes, but Jesus Christ, I didn't fucking kill her!"

"Mr. Reynolds, I need you to stand and face the wall," Brownlee instructed, voice flat with routine.

Van's gaze locked onto Prince, a drowning man spotting a distant shore. "This is a fucking set up. You know it is."

Prince stepped closer, his shadow falling across Van's face. "All I know is you're a thirty-year-old volleyball coach who lives alone and likes to fuck teenage girls. You're not irresponsible. You're a piece of shit," Prince said, voice chilled to sub-zero. "I would tread lightly, Mr. Reynolds. And in the meantime, I would begin to mull over a new vocation."

As Brownlee secured the handcuffs, Van's composure finally disintegrated completely. Tears streamed down his face, his body shaking with sobs.

"Please," he begged. "Please listen to me. I didn't kill her. Someone's setting me up. Why would I take that photo and then send it to the FBI? Think about it! Why would I do that?!"

Prince turned to Wilbur, dismissing Van as though he'd already faded from existence. "I'll be back at the motel."

But as Prince reached the door, he paused, struck by the raw desperation in Van's voice. The man was terrified. Not just of arrest, but of something else. Something he couldn't articulate. Prince had seen enough guilty men to know their patterns, the way they bargained and rationalized and minimized.

Van wasn't doing any of that.

"Who else knew about you and Evelyn?" Prince asked suddenly, turning back.

Van blinked through his tears. "What?"

"Who else knew? Think carefully."

"Nobody. We were very discreet." Van swallowed hard. "Except..."

"Except what?"

"About a month before she left for college, we were at my place. Someone knocked on the door. When I checked, no one was there. But there was a note."

"What did it say?"

Van took a moment to respond, the soft clinking of his cuffs filling the tense silence. "It said *I know*."

"And you never found out who left it?"

Van shook his head. "I thought it was kids pulling a prank."

Prince studied him for a long moment, then nodded to Brownlee, having obtained what he needed. "Take him."

As they led Van away, Prince lingered in the empty interrogation room, staring at the Polaroid still sealed in its evidence bag. Something about the whole setup felt wrong. The convenience of the photo arriving precisely when they needed a break, the too-neat packaging of Van Reynolds, a blubbering pussy with underage skeletons in his closet, as their killer.

He picked up the photograph, examining the handwritten. *18th BIRTHDAY* scrawled in the corner. The penmanship was distinctive. Bold, with an unusual slant to the letters. Prince made a mental note to compare it to samples from every person of interest in the case.

Because someone wanted Van Reynolds to take the fall for Evelyn Armstrongs murder.

And Prince was beginning to suspect that someone. Or something. Was clocking their every move.

The arrest of Van Reynolds mostly flew under the radar. Not due to lack of significance. Not because it wasn't reasonable to an extent.

Because it didn't last that long.

Four hours after Van Reynolds was released from custody, he sat in his car in the empty parking lot of Bronxville High, hands trembling on the steering wheel of his 2010 Toyota Camry. The ordeal had been humiliating. Handcuffed and hauled off in front of the faculty, thrown in a cell, questioned for hours about Evelyn Armstrongs murder.

And that Polaroid. Jesus Christ. He never should have taken it. Never should have crossed that line with a student, no matter how willing she seemed, how adult she appeared. He had known better. And now it had nearly cost him everything.

The school board had immediately placed him on administrative leave pending an investigation into his "inappropriate relationship" with a former student. His reputation was in tatters. The whispers had already started. Parents calling each other, students exchanging texts. Even if he was cleared of any involvement in Evelyn's death, his career was over.

But that wasn't what occupied his thoughts this morning.

Last night, while he was being processed for release, he'd received a text from Amber, a junior on the volleyball team who'd been sending him increasingly explicit messages over the past month. She wanted to meet. Said she "needed someone to talk to" about what had happened to Evelyn.

He knew he should ignore it. Block her number. Report her to guidance. But something in him. The same weakness that had led him to Evelyn. Made him respond: *Baseball field parking lot. 12 A.M.*

Now he waited, his stomach churning with equal parts anticipation and self-loathing. Just one more time, he told himself. One last taste before he left town for good.

He checked his watch: 12:02 AM. He drummed his fingers on the steering wheel, scanning the empty lot for signs of Amber's blue Honda Civic. Nothing yet.

The knock came from behind him.

Richard Armstrong sat in the backseat. Ski mask pulled over cold eyes. .45 caliber pistol leveled at the back of Van's head. The sound of leather stretching around the grip.

"Jesus Christ!" Van gasped, instinctively raising his hands. "Mr. Armstrong—"

"You like fucking people's daughters?" Richard's voice

was as calm as if he were asking about the weather. He threw an iPhone wrapped in a fuzzy pink case into the shotgun seat, the landing awakening a lock screen of Amber and some friends in white volleyball uniforms.

"Please," Van babbled, cold sweat breaking out across his forehead. "I had nothing to do with what happened to Evelyn. I swear to God—"

"I know," Richard said, his expression unchanging. "You're a run-of-the-mill pervert. Not a killer."

Van's relief was momentary. "Then why—"

"Because men like you don't stop," Richard interrupted. "They just get more careful. Move to another town. Find another school. Another girl."

"No, I've learned my lesson," Van pleaded, tears streaming down his face now. "I'm leaving town. Starting over. I'll never teach again—"

"You're right," Richard said, cocking the hammer of the .45 with a precise click. "You *won't* teach again."

Van's eyes widened. "Please, God, no—"

The explosion was deafening in the enclosed space of the Camry. Van's head snapped forward into his horn, the windshield painted with red mist.

Richard sat motionless in the backseat, ears ringing from the gunshot, watching the blood drip down the glass as the horn blared with finality. There was no relief. No satisfaction. No justice. It just... was. Everything was now.

He exited the car carefully, wiping down any surfaces he might have touched.

School would start in eight hours.

CHAPTER FOURTEEN

PRINCE, PRINCE, PRINCE

DECEMBER 6, 2022

Joyce Beckford stomped through the cold Bronxville night like a goddamn ghost, her cheap heels snapping like gunshots against the cracked sidewalk. Two in the morning, and the whole town was dead except for her.

Joyce wasn't like the others—she still had that glow, the kind of beauty that hadn't been ground down yet. Her cheeks were flushed from the cold, the early December air biting at her fair skin as she haunted the frozen streets. Her blonde hair, though a little tangled from the wind, still fell in soft waves down her shoulders, framing a face that didn't need the dime-store makeup she slathered on.

She wasn't rough, not yet, but the eyeliner was a bit too thick, the lipstick a shade too bright, like she was trying to look older, more experienced. Her parka, a faded green with faux fur trimming the hood, wasn't enough to keep her warm, but it hung on her slim frame just right, making her look almost fashionable if you squinted past the worn-out boots and the fact she was walking the streets at this hour. There was a freshness to her still, a softness in her eyes that didn't belong here. She had the kind of face men remembered—young, with lips just naturally a little pouty, skin smooth despite the bitter cold gnawing at her.

In the distance, a set of headlights cut through the early morning fog, rolling toward her slowly. She knew the routine, even if she was relatively new to it. She stopped under a streetlight, leaning casually against the pole, her eyes sharp, lips parting slightly in that way that men seemed to like. Her heart pounded beneath her parka, a nervous thrum, but she kept her face calm, her movements slow and deliberate, like she'd been here a thousand times before.

But she hadn't. Not really.

Not at all.

The vehicle revealed itself to be a black Chevrolet Caprice. Joyce assumed a 1983, being the daughter of a Newark grease monkey. It rolled into the curb slow and smooth. Joyce stood there, shifting on her feet, her toes nearly numb. She watched it pull up, the tumble of the engine soft, almost polite, like the driver knew how to move through the night without stirring it too much.

The window slid down with a quiet hum. Warm air spilled out, smelling of leather and something faintly sweet. The man leaned just far enough for her to catch the edge of his smile.

"You look cold," he said, his voice easy, like he was asking her if she wanted a drink or offering her a smoke. Friendly, casual, but with a weight beneath it. Joyce offered a smile, just enough to keep it professional, but not too much. She'd learned to measure those out carefully.

"Yeah. Cold night." She tucked a strand of blonde hair behind her ear, feeling the sting of wind on her bare skin. "You looking for company?"

"Depends. Are you good company?"

"Haven't gotten any complaints."

He chuckled softly, his eyes twinkling with a kind of charm that made her relax. His hand rested on the steering wheel, fingers drumming lazily. Joyce had seen a lot of types. The nervous ones, the mean ones, the ones who simply tried to pretend they weren't doing what they were doing. But this guy didn't fit any of those. He seemed calm; maybe too calm for this time of night. His voice had a soothing quality, like he was used to making people feel comfortable. He was handsome in that clean-cut, All-American way. Polished.

"Come on in," he said. "You'll freeze out there."

Joyce hesitated, then climbed in.

Heat swallowed her as she slipped into the passenger seat. The man—he'd introduced himself as Jake—pulled back onto the empty street.

"So, Joyce," Jake said, his eyes flicking to her briefly before settling back on the road. "What's a girl like you doing out in these streets? You seem—I dunno—too good for 'em."

The line was clumsy, but not crude. She shrugged, though his words warmed her in a way she hadn't expected.

"Girl's gotta make a living."

"I hear you," he said softly. "But you could do better than this."

There was a quiet sincerity in his voice that made her

want to believe him, if only for a moment. She glanced out the window, watching the streetlights blur past.

"Yeah. Maybe."

The silence between them was easy—almost comfortable. But as they drove farther from the center of town, the streets growing darker and more deserted, something in Joyce's gut twisted. They were heading *out* of town now, away from the lights, away from the places she knew. The warmth of the car started to feel less inviting, and more like a trap.

"So," she said, her voice steady but cautious, "where we going?"

Jake didn't miss a beat. "Someplace quiet," he said smoothly, his smile still there, but now it felt like a mask, something too perfect. "We'll get away from it all."

Her heart quickened, that instinct kicking in again, the one that told her something was off. She glanced at him from the corner of her eye, that charming smile still fixed in place, his hands steady on the wheel. He didn't *look* dangerous—nothing about him screamed trouble—but there was a coldness in his calm that sent a chill down her spine.

"Actually, Jake," she said, trying to keep her tone light, "maybe we could just stop here somewhere. I prefer to keep close."

The man chuckled again, but this time it was foreign, devoid of any sincerity, any heart.

It was airless and cruel.

"That's not my name, you fucking whore."

The snowfall thickened as Frankie Lopez lit another cigarette with numb fingers. The air stank of booze and smoke and sidewalk salt. He leaned against the brick wall behind the bar, hoodie soaked through, the whiskey in his gut barely warming him. Bronxville was dead quiet. Not a soul on the streets. It felt like the whole world was paused. Frozen in that moment between last call and first light.

He flicked the cigarette and crushed it under his boot, eyes twitching through the dark. This wasn't just a late-night wander. Frankie was hunting—chasing glass, the kind that quieted the gnaw and kept the dreams away.

He blinked into the dark across the parking lot and saw a shape.

A man. Covered head-to-toe in black, wearing a red-and-white hockey mask.

Frankie stared. The mask gleamed faintly under the streetlamp, scuffed and scratched, like it had been worn a hundred times before. The man's hands were gloved. Black leather ones from the mall. His shoulders were broad, torso slim but long.

Frankie flicked the cigarette and scoffed. "What, you a fucking ghost or something? You trying to scare me?"

The man didn't answer. Didn't speak. Just kept walking until he was a few feet away, boots crunching in the slush.

Frankie looked him up and down. No weapon. No words.

"This some kind of covert faggot shit? 'Cause I don't roll that way, bro. No disrespect."

The stranger didn't answer.

Didn't flinch.

Just drew a thin telescopic baton, steel flashing under the moonlight, and snapped it open—full-length, full intent.

Frankie's smirk faltered.

The first swipe hissed through the air. Frankie dodged it, then tried to pivot. Too slow. The next whipped low, sweeping his legs out from under him. Wet asphalt met spine with a wet thud, breath gone.

The baton crashed down again. And again. Ribs, kidney, hip. Precise, targeted strikes, the rhythm of someone who'd drilled this in mirrors. Frankie curled, forearms up, but the rod hammered through his guard until metal finally snapped with a flat, conclusive sound. A shard clattered away.

Silence. About a heartbeat, just the winter wind whistling softly between slush underfoot and the haunting ambience of a Bruce Springsteen record echoing from an apartment patio either too close to notice or too far removed to have anything to do with it.

Then the man knelt, fists uncaged. The first punch split Frankie's cheek; the second drove bone against teeth. Blood throbbed in his ears while the world pinwheeled red, and the night settled into the steady percussion of knuckles breaking him apart.

Frankie tried to scramble up, but a gloved hand yanked him by the hoodie and flung him into the side of a dumpster with sick force.

Stars. His vision flared white. Blood flooded his mouth.

Still, he laughed.

A low, gurgled chuckle bubbled out of him like tar.

The man paused mid-swing. Frankie spat a red string across the snow and grinned up at him, teeth pink and eyes wild.

"You hit like a fucking pussy."

That earned him a boot to the gut. He curled inward but kept laughing.

Another punch. This time to the temple. Frankie slumped sideways into the slush, head spinning, his maniacal laughter just sharp gasps of pain at this point.

The man hovered over him now, breath ragged through the holes of the mask. Steam rising. One hand clenched, the other trembling.

Frankie coughed and smiled again.

"You're not done, are you?" Frankie taunted. "Came all the way here to kill me. Do it, you little bitch!"

The man just stood there. Statue-still, head tilted like a curious animal. After a while, he knelt. Leaned in. Frankie caught the scent. Rubber, cheap cologne, blood—and beneath it all, *sulfur*. Like something crawled out of Hell just to take a closer look.

Then the voice came. Low, smooth, dripping in black tar.

"You know what her last words were?"

Frankie's smile twitched.

"My baby."

The man's eyes, cold and eerily vacant, wrinkled behind the mask—a smile. Frankie held his gaze as the man stood, satisfied, and walked away.

Frankie blinked up at the snowfall. Let the blood run down his jaw. He shot upright, clutching his midsection with an awful scream.

"What, you're not gonna finish it? Come on, tough guy!" he called out, coughing up blood. "You motherfucker! Come back here, you motherfucker! Fuck you! You don't have the balls or something? Come here, you fuck!"

The man paused at the edge of the lot. Frankie knew if this asshole came back he was probably dead. But he remembered the Kershaw sitting in his back pocket, and if Frankie was going to die of internal bleeding, he would at least *try* to take this piece of shit with him.

But he left.

Frankie listened to the footsteps fade out.

Then he passed out.

6:27 A.M.

Daybreak.

Prince's service weapon sat in its shoulder holster on the table beside his keys, a Thai takeout box, and another polished pint of booze.

There were then three knocks at the door.

"Hello?" Prince called, monotone.

"It's me," Wilbur said.

Prince groaned, hawked, spat somewhere, and swung his foot onto the floor, zombie-walked to the door, and opened it. It was another gray morning. Wilbur was dressed to the nines and holding two cups of coffee.

"Dead girl at the park. Some medieval shit," Wilbur said plainly. "Got you nonfat."

"Irrigation worker called it in around five in the morning," Nichols said. "Awful thing, ain't it?"

The frost on the grass hadn't even sweated off by the

time the SD finished setting up camp at Bronxville Recreational Park. Joyce Beckford—what remained of her—lay sprawled on the cold ground, abdomen slashed open vertically, intestines partially exposed. Her face was caked in dry blood, beaten beyond recognition, eyes staring skyward. Just like Evelyn.

Prince made his way over to Nichols and Brownlee at the perimeter while the forensic team worked the scene.

"Haller?" Prince asked.

"Not in yet," Brownlee replied. "He'll love this, won't he?"

"He's a big boy," Prince said. "And he ain't the one lying there."

"Lacerations detected on the back. Flip!" one of the white coats called out. His peer nodded, and the two began carefully rolling the body.

Prince and the others watched in silence. Halfway through, Prince caught a glint. Something unnatural.

The tech leaned in, squinting. "Is that... a fuckin' poem?"

"Just written with a hunting knife," Brownlee said. Nichols made the sign of the cross.

Prince approached gingerly. He crouched next to the corpse, scanning the jagged lines carved into her back. Four uneven bars, deep enough to put her on a ventilator if she'd lived:

Prince, Prince, Prince
You rode in on your horse
Fell for the kid fucker and his fingerprints
Here's another corpse

Prince's breath snagged. For a moment his face didn't move at all, but his jaw trembled like it wanted to lock. He rubbed at his scruff, fingertips raw against skin. His pulse hammered in his ears, louder than the camera shutters, louder than the rustle of plastic.

His own name, carved into the back of a murdered girl. Not taunting the FBI. Not the town. *Him.*

He rose stiffly, almost in slow motion, as though standing too fast would give it more power. Behind him the chatter kept going—clinical, detached. Prince heard none of it. Just that refrain repeating in his head, already burned into memory.

Finally, his voice tore out—hoarse, too sharp, hiding nothing:

"Get Haller on the fucking phone," he barked, striding off. "He still in bed? Jesus Christ. Move!"

As Prince stormed back to the car, his thoughts raced in jagged, overlapping loops. The killer had been watching them. Not just following their work, but dissecting it. Studying them, like a butcher learns the anatomy of his stock. He knew they'd bring in Reynolds. And now he was flaunting his lead. Killing another young woman just to prove he could.

What sickened Prince most was the realization that if they'd moved faster, connected the dots sooner, Joyce Beckford might still be alive. Her death was his.

He slammed his fist against the passenger dash, the pain barely registering through his rage.

"James," Wilbur said, climbing into the driver's seat. "This isn't your fault."

Prince grunted. Wordless, dismissive.

"We'll get him," Wilbur insisted. "He's taunting. We've

seen this before—"

"Yeah?" Prince snapped, turning. "You ever see your name carved into a dead woman, Wilbur?"

"I—no—"

"Then don't fucking say shit like that!"

Prince looked back toward the scene, a muscle flexing in his cheek. "This fucking town. It chews people up and acts surprised when they bleed."

Wilbur didn't say anything for a moment.

Then, evenly: "I'm on your side, James. Always. But don't *ever* fucking speak to me like that."

Prince stared out the windshield. Then gave a small, silent nod.

The heater rattled softly. The engine idled.

The silence between them wasn't angry. Just full.

After a moment, Wilbur's voice pierced the veil, quiet but clear: "Van Reynolds is dead."

Prince blinked. "You're kidding."

"Shot in his car. Midnight. Back of the head. Looked like a clean hit."

Prince didn't say anything.

"And Frankie Lopez is in the ICU. Someone beat him half to death near the bar after close. Witness found him unconscious in the snow around 2:32 A.M. EMT says he's lucky he didn't freeze solid."

Prince buried his face in his hands.

"Jesus *Christ*," he said. "Is this a fucking group project now?"

Wilbur gave a dry chuckle. "You want to delegate?"

"I want to *resign*. Give my badge to Nichols. Let him feed it to his dog."

Wilbur smiled, staring at his lap. They sat in silence for a while, listening to the soft thrum of the heater.

Finally, Wilbur: "What do you want to do?"

"Take me to the hospital."

"We talking to Frankie?"

"Just me," Prince said, flat. "You take the scene at the school."

Wilbur clocked the look in his eyes and knew better than to argue.

As they pulled away from the curb, snow spiraled down in slow, indifferent waves. The crime scene faded in the rearview, swallowed by fog and red tape.

And still, Prince couldn't shake the feeling. The weight of something unseen, but watching.

A presence tucked inside the edges of the frame.

A name he hadn't heard yet, but would never forget.

The face in the crowd.

Frankie lay motionless, eyelids cracked. One eye gone completely red. Breathing shallow around cracked ribs. He clocked Prince's silhouette and tried to push upright. *Failed.*

"Easy," Prince said, voice low. "You move, the tape in your lung folds up. Let the nurses earn their pay."

Frankie swallowed. "Who are you?"

"James Prince. FBI."

A beat. "You're Evelyn's Fed."

"And you're the kid who keeps catching ass-whuppings instead of answers." Prince eased onto the visitor chair by the IV pole. "I need your head clear for five minutes. Think you can manage?"

Frankie's laugh rattled, devolved into coughs. "You kidding? My head feels like a fucking jukebox someone took a bat to."

"Good. Means you're alive. Listen." Prince leaned forward, eyes foxbright even under hospital fluorescents. "Who did this to you?"

"I didn't see his face. Tall fucker, though. Moved like he'd done it a hundred times." Frankie's gaze drifted to the ceiling. "Had a baton. Thin, steel, like a prison guard's. Broke it on me before he switched to fists."

"Anything else?"

Frankie played with his bracelet, eyes low. "He, uh... at the end, he said something to me... about Evelyn's last words."

Prince stared.

"And?"

Frankie didn't answer.

Just looked up. Eyes hollow, reflective. The kind of stare you get after experiencing something that doesn't leave when you close your eyes. When your throat locks up, like it's trying to spare the rest of the world.

Prince knew instantly. Whether it was shared telepathy, instinct, or just the weight of it pressing through the quiet—he knew. And for once, he let the unspeakable be just that.

Unspoken.

He cleared his throat. Tapped the IV pole. "One more thing, Frankie. Off record. What the fuck were you doing out there at 2:00 A.M.?"

Silence. Frankie stared at the wall clock, ashamed. Finally: "I was supposed to meet a guy for some crank. Haven't wanted to sleep lately. I get these dreams." He shook his head. "I know it's stupid. Bad habits die slower than people, right?"

Prince sat back, studying the swollen kid for a long, quiet moment. Something like fondness flickered in his eyes. The corners of his mouth flirted with a smirk.

"You're not afraid of anything, huh?" he said, less a question than it was recognition.

Frankie managed a lopsided grin through split lips. "Just you."

Prince smiled. "Smartass." He stood up. "No more alley runs or I'll finish you off. You got me?"

Frankie nodded. "Yes, sir."

Prince slid a business card onto the tray beside the untouched cup of ice chips.

"When the swelling goes down and we're past all this shit," he said, "give me a call."

He turned for the door, leaving Frankie chuckling softly at the ceiling.

Richard Armstrong was out of booze.

The empty Jameson fifth sat on the coffee table like a crime scene prop—smudged, sticky, hollow. The house smelled of old leather, dust, and loss. Shadows pressed into the corners like mold. He didn't look upstairs. Janet hadn't been awake in days. Pills, steam, static TV, that wheezy tape deck rewinding the same three VHS tapes until the audio warped. If she spoke, it was in sleep. If she moved, he didn't notice.

Sometimes he saw Van in the hall near the coatrack. Smiling. Not smug. Patient. Like he knew Richard was catching up. Waiting.

He stood, knees creaking, body stiff from too many

nights on the recliner. His body wanted to rot. He wanted whiskey.

He grabbed his keys and coat. The house made no sound as he left it. No goodbye. No warning. Just silence thick enough to chew.

Snow came down hard. Big flakes. Slow. It blanketed the street and trees, the front steps. A clean white death mask. Richard trudged through it, boots crunching once he hit the driveway.

His truck groaned awake, spat heat into the cab. He caught himself in the rearview—red-eyed, beard patchy, cheeks sunken.

He didn't look away.

The liquor store sat in the neighborhood like a tumor no one had the guts to cut out. Irish-owned. Still clinging to that same flag-waving, grimy pride since Kennedy got his head turned inside out. Richard parked sharp against the curb, tires scraping frostbitten asphalt, the brake shrieking like a gutted deer. He stepped out slow, every joint in his body aching like old sins.

Inside, it stank of stale mop water, wet cardboard, and desperation. Behind the counter stood a boy who thought he was a man: Jack McGregor, twenty-nine, plugged into the void by way of a single AirPod, thumbs dancing on a phone. Jets jersey, empty eyes. Useless.

"Case of Jameson," Richard muttered, pulling out his wallet with a motion like drawing a weapon.

"Richard?"

The voice didn't belong there. It was too warm. Too

bright. Like a candle lit in a crypt.

He turned.

The man who stood there could've given Clooney a run for his money. Tall, sun-touched, that perfect suburban jawline and unthreatening charisma that hid in plain sight. A JV football coach, maybe. Or the type of guy who taught Sunday school before hitting the bar to cheat on his wife.

He held up a six-pack of Coors like it was some kind of peace offering.

"Billy Baker," he said, all teeth and sunshine. "I've been hoping to run into you."

"Yeah," Richard said, voice low. "Long time."

The smile faltered for just a moment, like a frame catching in a projector. Then his voice sank into a sermon's cadence, the kind of borrowed gravity men use when they want their words mistaken for empathy.

"What happened with Evie..." The name dropped between them like a stone into still water. "Christ, Richard. What a disgrace."

There it was. *Evie*. Rolled out like he had a right to it. Richard felt something shift in his gut. A quiet rupture, like a fault line threatening to split wide.

"Thanks," he said, flat.

Billy stepped in closer, breath warm with beer and something fouler underneath. "She was a good one, huh? Special girl. I remember her well. Sharp, sweet, always looking out for the quiet kids."

Richard stared at him. *Through* him, really.

"She wasn't sweet."

Billy's head tilted, eyes still bright. "No?"

"No," Richard said, jaw tight. "You're thinking of someone else."

For exactly three beats, the mask slipped. Something

cold and hungry stared through the eyes before the Sunday school smile slid back into place, polished and perfect.

"Well, you'd know best."

The air between them thickened. Not tense. Not awkward. Loaded. Two predators arriving at the same watering hole.

Billy exhaled, all false camaraderie. "Well, I should get going. And listen: if you or the wife need anything, anything at all—you know where to find me. Everyone does, I suppose."

Richard nodded. "Appreciated."

Billy turned and walked out without another word, strutting with the easy gait of a man who hadn't buried a fucking thing in his life.

Richard stood there, keys in one hand, wallet in the other. Breath shallow. Eyes restless. He leaned on the counter.

"That teacher ever been in here before?"

Jack looked up, finally unplugging from his digital coma. "Huh? I don't know, man."

Richard took his case of Jameson.

At the truck he froze.

Van Reynolds sat in the passenger seat—one eye gone, bone cratered, jaw slack, crimson soaking his collar.

Richard blinked once.

Twice.

Gone.

Just an empty seat.

It was only upon climbing into his truck that something occurred to Richard.

William Baker never called himself Billy.

And the son of a bitch didn't drink.

Three days since he'd spoken to Jennifer. Maybe four. Prince couldn't remember anymore. Her texts lingered unanswered on his phone like accusations.

You good? Just call me when you can. James, this is getting old.

He left his phone on the nightstand at the Westchester lodge and walked into town. Cold air bit his face. Good. Maybe it would clear his head.

The Flailing Crab was nothing special. Neon beer signs. Broken jukebox. Ceiling tiles stained the color of old promises. But the whiskey poured strong and the bartender kept quiet. And that was enough.

Three drinks in, she appeared. Black hair pulled back tight against her skull. Leather jacket that had seen better places than this. Eyes that calculated more than they revealed.

"Mind if I sit?"

He nodded at the empty stool. "Free country."

"Marisol," she said.

"James."

Their glasses met with a dull click.

She drew him out like poison from a wound. By drink three, he was spilling everything. Frankie's beating, Armstrong unraveling, Joyce Beckford, the whole case collapsing like wet cardboard.

"Ever feel like the deeper you dig," Prince said, "the more it feels like you're standing in your own grave?"

Marisol's smile was floss-thin. "What if the grave isn't yours?"

He laughed. A hollow sound.

They left together.

Morning light sliced through the blinds. Prince's head throbbed in time with his shoulder. His mouth tasted of bourbon and bad decisions.

A soft click.

Marisol sat in the armchair by the window, fully dressed. A small black recorder rotated between her fingers.

His own voice played back: "*—father's a wreck. SEAL background. All-American meltdown. Girl caught in the crossfire. Something doesn't add up. Might be the boyfriend. Might be the father. Feels like both.*"

Prince stood. "Turn that off."

She did.

"I was going to tell you—"

"You fucking recorded me?"

"I'm a reporter." She stood. "Marisol Reyes. *New York Sentinel.*"

He stared at her. "You set me up."

One eyebrow lifted. "Come on, James. You're a grown man. You drank, you got drunk, you talked. You didn't say anything that wasn't true."

"Delete it."

She handed him a business card instead. Silver lettering gleamed in the half-light.

MARISOL REYES, INVESTIGATIVE REPORTER
The New York Sentinel

"I'm heading back to the city. Don't worry. Nothing prints without checking in."

"We're done."

She paused at the door, lips curved slightly. "Maybe. Or maybe I'll see you around. Maybe I'll even run into Jennifer. You should really text her back, by the way. She might think something happened."

She shot him a wink. The door closed just as the clock Prince beamed would've connected with her smug face. Instead, it shattered into a million plastic shards, scattering across the floor like every other bad joke this town had tried on him.

He studied her card.

Then crushed it in his fist.

CHAPTER FIFTEEN

YOU NEVER KNOW THE LAST TIME...

DECEMBER 8, 2022

Nineteen days.

Nineteen days since Evelyn Armstrong vanished in the dead of night. Seventeen since Twin Lakes gave her back. And nothing. Cooped up in The Flailing Crab with Wilbur at 6:00 P.M., Prince rubbed his temples, the phantom scent of iron and rain still clinging to him. It wasn't real, just a trick of the mind, but it stuck anyway. Blood always did.

Here's another corpse.

Two murders now.

Two victims, worlds apart but forever linked in tragedy.

In theory, Van Reynolds should have been the one. It had taken mere hours to match the prints on the film to Reynolds and just minutes for him to confess to what the

Polaroid had already implied. *Yes*, he'd been intimate with Evelyn. And *yes*, he knew it was wrong. But murder?

It hadn't really fit. And then the second body popped up while Reynolds was cooling his heels in lockup. Joyce Beckford, the sex worker with zero connection to Evelyn Armstrong. Or to Reynolds, for that matter. The timing had forced Prince's hand. Reynolds walked.

Then there was Frankie Lopez. Evelyn's ex, dragged in on a tide of anger and circumstantial evidence. But he was nowhere near the second murder. He'd been getting the shit kicked out of him by a baton-swinging lunatic near The Flailing Crab, just as Joyce Beckford was caught on a neighbor's grainy Ring cam climbing into a vintage black car. Specifically, a 1983 Chevrolet Caprice.

Prince only knew one word for this shit.

Chaos.

Two, actually. *Fucking chaos*.

Wilbur came over with two sweating Budweiser's, set them down, and slid across from his brooding partner.

Prince made a face. "Fuck is this?"

"Beer," Wilbur said. "You've got enough bourbon in you to pickle half of Salt Lake City. Time to hydrate."

"Keeping count?"

Wilbur raised an eyebrow. "Are you?"

Prince glared but drank. "M.E.?"

"Killer used a six-inch hunting knife," Wilbur said. "Non-serrated. Carvings applied post-mortem. Woman's name was Joyce Anna Beckford. Low-level prostitute, rats nest outside town."

"Was she raped?"

Wilbur shook his head. "Evidence of sex, DNA pending, but no real indication she was forced upon by anyone," Wilbur said, "and certainly not within the window of abduction. Plus, the killer used a condom with Evelyn."

"Because this wasn't about control," Prince said. "Wasn't even about killing. This was a message. Planting Van's prints on the picture? That wasn't a frame job. It was a power move. He wanted to rock the boat and waste our time doing it."

"Might be developing an ego," Wilbur said. "Could get sloppy."

"Or more dangerous," Prince said. "He's feeding on it. The attention. The fear."

"The hate."

"We keep playing into it, and he'll escalate."

"Unless we catch him first."

Prince shook his head. "Depends on what drives him. If it's ego, notoriety pushes him into the light. If it's control, he'll burrow deeper. Either way, he's ahead of us."

Wilbur crossed his arms and let a gust of air out through his nose.

"What?"

"Who've you really interacted with out here, man? Anyone stand out?"

Prince's brow furrowed, his mind flicking past the one who'd extracted more than just case details from him. "Jonathan Evans."

Wilbur raised an eyebrow. "The reporter?"

"He's been hanging around," Prince said with a shrug. "Working some angle. He was taking pictures of the car while we were eating breakfast yesterday."

"Huh. What did he want?"

"Collaboration. Said he might have something."

"You believe him? Or you think he's just pulling for the spotlight?"

"I don't know. Anything new on Richard?"

"Still a ghost. The wife's holding things together. Starting to put on makeup, go out to the grocery store. But he's locked himself in entirely, save a run to the liquor store. Guy's grieving." Wilbur shrugged and popped a peanut into his mouth.

"Maybe." Prince pulled out a photo from the case file. Richard Armstrong in his Navy SEAL uniform. Eyes cold, resolute. The kind of face that gave nothing away.

"Or he's planning," Prince said. "Guys like this don't lie down and die. They act."

Before Wilbur could answer, a shadow fell across the table.

Jonathan Evans stood there, camera slung, bookbag heavy on his shoulder.

"Special Agent Prince," Evans said. "What's the special tonight? Justice on the half shell?"

Prince sighed. "What do you want?"

"I know the FBI's not much for small talk," Evans said, sliding into the booth uninvited, "but I thought I'd check in. You know, see how the feds are enjoying their time in the country—"

"Evans—"

"You two want to hear me out, or would you rather sit here drinking horse piss and staring at your phones like a couple of broads?"

Prince glared. "You got five minutes."

"I'll do it in three," Evans said, hoisting his bookbag onto the table with a thud. "Miley McDermott. Seventeen. Went missing earlier last month. Every river to Timbuktu dragged, every bush ruffled—"

"We're familiar."

"You're familiar, sure, but what you're not familiar with is that Miley McDermott's last verified sighting was a click shy of a garage in Yonkers called Baker Auto Works," Evans said, tapping the folder proudly. "Family-owned. Run by one Morris Baker, ex-con. Got out in '94 after doing eight years for aggravated assault and attempted murder. All the old prick does now is fix cars on the North end and pound the bottle. Now, the kid's friend said Miley liked to sneak out sometimes. Head up to Yonkers, meet older guys, maybe score some blow. The garage? Right in the same area. But here's where it gets good."

He spread a photocopy of a yearbook page.

"Billy Baker. Bronxville's beloved biology teacher. Car nut. Restores rides out of his dad's garage on weekends, sometimes his own." He pointed to Prince. "Beckford entered a Caprice the night she was taken, right? Things were hot in the eighties, right when pops got out of the pen. Billy's been seen driving his little projects around town for years, according to locals."

Wilbur exhaled through his nose. "Circumstantial."

"Sure," Evans said. "But Billy's last school in Rochester let him go for 'inappropriate behavior.' A student disappeared for a week."

Prince's tone was flat. "A week?"

"Girl turned up safe. Police wrote it off as a runaway. But she never went back to school. Neither did Baby Billy. Instead, he gets shuffled south to Bronxville like nothing happened."

Prince and Wilbur exchanged a glance.

"C'mon, fellas." Evans gestured at the folder. "McDermott vanishes near the family garage. Armstrong, one of his former students, raped and slaughtered. Beckford? Lured into the same Caprice that could've rolled straight out of dad's shop."

Prince leaned back, drumming his fingers against the

beer bottle.

Wilbur asked, "Why bring this to us instead of printing it?"

"Because I don't have enough."

"And what do you get out of it?" Prince asked.

Evans didn't hesitate. "The truth."

"You're not a cop."

Evans leaned forward. "You got kids, Agent Prince?"

Prince's guard slipped a notch. "Yeah. A little girl."

"I got two. Thirteen and fifteen. So what do I get out of this? A night's rest."

Prince studied him. Then opened the folder.

"If you're wrong, you're wasting time."

"If I'm right, you're already behind," Evans shot back.

"We're overdue at the high school," Prince said. "Good time to get a feel for the son before we ambush the father."

Evans lit a cigarette, smiling faintly. "Then I'll tell you right now, Prince Charming. You ain't gonna like him."

The hallways of Bronxville High had a strange hush, like the building itself was holding its breath. Dust motes floated in fractured beams of late-afternoon sunlight, and the polished floors gleamed like an endless mirror. Prince and Wilbur walked through the corridor, footsteps muted by air thick with the sterile tang of industrial cleaner. The smell clung to the nostrils, a ghost of maintenance that couldn't scrub away the rot beneath.

Prince thought about the girl they were here to discuss. Evelyn Armstrong. Everyone in this place had a story about her. Bright. Focused. Kind. The perfect student.

Teachers spoke her name with reverence usually reserved for eulogies. But the more Prince listened, the more it sounded like one written by people who never really knew the dead.

The Evelyn they described was a list of achievements. Honor roll. Soccer captain. Science fair champion. Ambitious. A *leader*. Impressive. But beneath the tributes lay cracks, faint outlines of a girl who was more than her résumé. Closed off. Guarded. The kind who let the world see what she wanted it to see, and kept the rest locked away.

It was late afternoon when Prince first saw William Baker. Hunched over a prep table in the biology wing, rearranging test tubes. His gray sweater hung loose over a solid frame, and the thin-rimmed Windsor glasses perched on his narrow nose reflected the overhead lights, hiding his eyes.

"Mr. Baker," Prince called.

Baker turned, his movements slow and deliberate, as though his body resisted the interruption. "Agents," he said, his voice smooth and radio-like. "Call me William. FBI, I assume?"

"Yep," Prince said. "Special Agent James Prince. That's Special Agent Christopher Wilbur, my partner. Evelyn Armstrong was a student of yours. Mind if we ask a few questions?"

"Not at all," Baker said, setting down a beaker with precision. "Though I'd have thought you'd be done by now. It's been nineteen days."

Prince's gaze tightened. "We're investigating another case tied to hers."

"Tragic," Baker said. "She was one of my best students."

"How would you describe her?" Wilbur asked.

"Focused," Baker said, savoring the word. "Driven. She

wasn't just good. She wanted to be the best. Soccer, science, exams—it didn't matter. She wanted to dominate. And she did."

"She rub anyone the wrong way?" Prince asked.

"Evelyn kept people at a distance. Careful about who she let in."

"Did she ever talk to you about feeling threatened?" Wilbur asked.

Baker tilted his head. "No. But she carried pressure. Her father had his expectations. If she didn't score on Saturday, you'd hear him a town over. Parents usually do that with sons, but..." Baker smirked, a glint of something almost gleeful in his eyes. "Some see kids as projects, don't they?"

Prince's stomach turned, though his face stayed neutral. There was *something* about the guy, something he couldn't name but couldn't ignore. Not just the way he spoke—careful, measured—but the way the room felt heavier in his presence. Like he'd sucked all the air into himself and left nothing for anyone else.

"Mind giving us your number?"

Baker nodded, took the notepad and pen. His left hand moved fluidly, neat and precise. As he passed it back, he smiled. A small, tight thing that didn't reach his eyes.

"Anything to help," he said. "You never know the last time you'll see someone, right?"

Prince felt his head tilt. "Sorry?"

"Life is fragile, Agent Prince. That's all. Now if you'll excuse me, I'm proctoring an AP test."

"Which one's yours?" Wilbur asked, pointing toward the staff lot below.

"The Prius," Baker said with pride. "Thing's lasted me for years. I'll run it into the ground."

"Lot of car guys drive Priuses?" Prince asked, eyes flat.

"We don't condemn efficiency, Agent Prince," Baker shot back with a half-smile, tone dripping with snark. "Take care, gentlemen."

Prince watched him leave, unease and disdain building in his chest like a pressure cooker.

Fucking guy.

"I don't like him," Prince said.

"No shit," Wilbur scoffed. "You leave your poker face back in the city? Look, he might be a prick. Weird as hell, too. But that doesn't mean he's out there killing young women."

"Yeah," Prince muttered, eyes still on the hall. "Yeah, maybe."

They left.

The air felt heavier.

CHAPTER SIXTEEN

AMBUSH

DECEMBER 10, 2022

The snow came down in thick sheets, coating the cracked pavement outside the garage in a deceptive stillness. Prince sat in the passenger seat, one hand resting on the grip of his sidearm, the other tapping against the door. Wilbur drove, his gaze fixed on the looming silhouette of Baker's Garage. Evans sat in the back, talking a mile a minute like he always did.

"I'm tellin' you, these two are no good," Evans muttered, breath fogging up the window. "Morris Baker's been a scumbag his whole life. Used to run with the Ghost Shadows back in the eighties. And the kid? Forget it! He's a fuckin' psycho."

Prince exhaled through his nose, unimpressed. The whole trip, Evans had been running his mouth, hadn't been able to shut the fuck up, about how this was *it*, how they were standing on the precipice of true crime immortality, how it was all over. Of course, he knew better. Prince, that is. Shit didn't work like that. There were no easy resolutions. No neat little bows.

He let him talk all the same, and then they were there.

The alleged "garage" was an old industrial bomb shelter of a space, rusted-out cars stacked on lifts, an eerie quiet humming in the cold. No lights on, no movement inside. The place was dead.

Just dead.

Evans let himself out. "I'll go knock. These guys know me."

Prince felt a frown form instantly. Something about this was wrong. Only then did it occur to Prince that they'd never confirmed *who* Evans had been corresponding with. He opened his mouth to say something, but Evans was already stepping over a low-hanging wire stretched across the—

BOOM!

A shockwave punched through Prince's chest and spiderwebbed the windshield as Evans was eviscerated, chunks of bone and viscera flung across the snow. Wilbur bailed and hit the ground first, rolling behind the car, and Prince followed instinctively, his ears ringing like a church bell struck too hard.

Then came the gunfire.

A turret-mounted machine gun in the corner of the garage roared to life, spitting bullets in a relentless arc. The windshield of the sedan exploded into shards, the hood rattling under the onslaught.

"MOVE!" Wilbur barked, yanking Prince by the collar.

They sprinted, diving behind a rusted-out truck frame.

More bullets chewed through the metal, inches from their skulls. Prince pulled out his gun, breath fogging in rapid bursts. They were pinned. Whoever set this up was two steps ahead, waiting for them.

Prince's mind worked fast. The turret was automated, motion-triggered. The shooter, if there was one, was inside.

"Cover me," he growled to Wilbur, then broke into a sprint.

He zig-zagged, ducking low, his heart hammering like a war drum. The turret adjusted its aim just a second too late. Prince dove through the shattered garage window, rolling hard onto the concrete floor. Silence swallowed him whole. Inside, it was dark. Reeked of motor oil, piss, and something worse.

He crept forward, gun raised. Past rows of tool benches, a stripped-down Malibu in the center of the space. He heard movement in the back. Heavy breathing. A wheezing groan.

Morris Baker sat slumped in a folding chair, hairless and booze-blotched, a needle still buried in his left arm. His jaundiced eyes were half-drained of life, the rest not far behind.

Prince stepped closer, gun steady. "Sir...?"

The old man lifted his head, retched up a mouthful of blood, then sagged back.

Prince scanned the workbench beside him. Scattered photographs of young girls, horrifically bound and brutalized. A dagger lay across them, its blade crusted in old blood. On the far wall, clothes. Tiny clothes. Miley McDermott's hoodie. Evelyn Armstrongs beanie.

Outside, he heard Wilbur shouting, backup sirens wailing in the distance.

"The devil," Morris croaked, then slumped forward, dead before he hit the floor.

Prince stood there in the dark, gun hanging by his hip now, staring down at Morris' defecating, farting corpse.

The backup arrived like a thundering cavalry, red and blue lights slicing through the snowfall. Prince didn't move. He stood still, the weight of what he'd uncovered pressing down harder than the cold ever could.

Wilbur climbed through the shattered window, gun still drawn. He stopped short at the carnage. Morris Baker's corpse slumped beside the blood-slick workbench, the grotesque gallery of trophy photographs staring back like a jury from Hell.

"Jesus Christ," Wilbur breathed, voice cracking. "What the fuck is this?"

Prince didn't answer. His gaze was locked on the tiny clothes pinned neatly to the wall. Fragments of childhood, of innocence, of lives erased. Silent screams woven into fabric. Every detail in this room whispered one thing: this wasn't just the lair of a killer. This was a shrine.

Evans was gone. Vaporized outside by a tripwire bomb that spoke of methodical, almost surgical cruelty. Prince had seen traps like that before, in war zones and terror cells. Not in the vicinity of white houses with crocheted curtains and neatly folded laundry.

Forensics would crawl this place for hours. They'd scrape the floors, swab every surface, photograph every inch. But Prince knew the truth was already evaporating. Whatever Morris Baker had been hiding died with him. And maybe that was the plan.

"We need to call it in," Wilbur said, barely above a whisper. "Full investigation. No exceptions."

Prince nodded slowly, but his thoughts raced. It all felt

too... perfect. The body. The photos. The trap rigged just in time for a witness. A monster caught red-handed and silenced in the same breath.

And Prince didn't believe in final acts. Not like this.

Something deeper was still breathing beneath all this blood and snow.

Outside, the snow picked up, swallowing the flashing lights and sirens, layering everything in quiet absolution. Soon, this place would vanish beneath a fresh white sheet, as if the earth itself was trying to forget.

Prince knew better. Evil doesn't end.

It just changes shape.

The glow from the monitor made his skin look pale and sickly, like a man rotting quietly from the inside out.

Richard sat motionless at his desk, hands resting on the keyboard without moving. The office was still. Quiet enough to hear the subtle hum of the baseboard heater, the occasional tick of drywall expanding with the night. The walls were bare except for a single framed photo of Evelyn, maybe nine years old, holding a Halloween pumpkin like she hadn't seen darkness yet.

The forum post sat open in front of him.

Username: aeonhelix11. No avatar. No follow-up. No reply feature. The body of the message burned in his head: *Manny Alvarez. Also known as 'Gold.' Pills, meth, girls. Greenlakes, Senior Ditch Day 2022. Evelyn looked uncomfortable. Frankie almost fought him. Yonkers, West Side. Blue tarp fence. House watches you back.*

It didn't feel like a lead.

It felt like a dare.

Richard had been in rooms with men who lied before they spoke. The wording in the post had that same quiet urgency. Too detailed to dismiss, but something about it tried too hard to earn his trust. He didn't believe in trust. Not anymore.

Still... the photo was real.

The attachment sat open in another encrypted tab. Manny's arm around Evelyn. Frankie off to the side, half-scowling. Evelyn with that hollowed-out body language. Smiling because someone told her to. A smile Richard had only seen once in real time, the week before she died.

The dark web was full of ghosts. But this one knew his name.

He hadn't moved in ten minutes. Just stared. Frozen between action and memory. *House watches you back.*

"I'm going to the drug store."

Janet. Standing in the doorway. Dressed like she was making an effort. Hair brushed. Lip gloss. Trying. For both of them.

"Are you out of your Zyprexa? I'll grab it."

Richard blinked. It took him a second to come back.

"Okay, honey," he said. Late. Offbeat. Like the words had to travel through fog. Hadn't even answered the damn question.

She hesitated. Studied him. She knew the difference between his silence and his trances. This was the latter. The cold one. The one that made her skin crawl and want to hug him at the same time.

"I'll be back in twenty," she said, something telling her to *leave it*. "You should eat something."

And then she was gone.

The door clicked shut.

Richard looked back at the screen. At the name: *Manny Alvarez.*

Little shit had a record. Had disappeared long enough to reappear as something worse.

The forum post told him what he wanted. But the internet didn't bleed. Didn't twitch. Didn't lie with fear in its voice.

If Manny was real, someone on the street would know. Someone who could confirm it in person. Someone scared enough to be honest.

He closed the laptop and stood. The chair creaked like it hadn't been moved in years.

Days had passed since the run-in with the lady reporter.

The heater in Prince's room rattled like something trapped and dying. Prince sat alone, watching shadows crawl across the wall.

The case was hemorrhaging.

Another young woman slaughtered. Reynolds dead. Evans in pieces. Richard coming undone.

He opened the nightstand drawer. The crumpled card. Smoothed it. Dialed.

"New York Sentinel, how may I direct your call?"

"Marisol Reyes."

Silence stretched like taffy.

"Hold."

Click.

A new voice. Male, clipped, East Coast. "Traynor, Metro Editor. Can I ask who's calling?"

Prince didn't waste time. "Marisol said she was headed back to the city."

"Last I heard, she was off to Westchester. Last week, I think?"

"She left Wednesday morning."

"Right." A pause. Prince could hear heavy fingers tapping a desk, gum being chewed. "Well. I haven't heard from her. No calls, no texts. I figured she got busy. Or cold feet."

"What was the story?"

"Half a paragraph in my inbox. Something about a federal homicide agent coming apart at the seams up in Westchester."

A beat. "Who exactly am I talking to?"

Prince hung up.

He didn't need to hear more.

He already knew.

PART THREE

MILEY

CHAPTER SEVENTEEN

TOUCH DARKNESS, AND DARKNESS TOUCHES YOU

She didn't know how long she'd been in the basement. The dark had gotten heavy. Thick, like a blanket soaked in something foul. The kind of dark that pressed against your eyeballs and made you forget what light felt like. Her throat was raw. Her legs ached. Her fingertips were scraped and swollen.

But she was still alive.

Miley whimpered quietly to herself, the way a child might sing in the dark just to keep the monsters confused. The concrete was cold under her bare feet. She didn't remember how she got here. Just that one day she woke up and the world had become this: a basement that didn't want to let her go. In the far corner, Prince stood motionless, half-draped in shadow. He couldn't move. Couldn't speak. Just watched, helpless, as if trapped behind the glass of his own mind.

She found a box. Then another. Water-damaged cardboard, soft at the corners, but they stacked. Wobbly, but they held. She kept going. Barely breathing. Her hands shook.

The vent was up near the ceiling. Twelve feet, maybe more. Too high for someone like her.

But still, she climbed. Up the boxes. One foot, then the next. Hands gripping the edges.

Fingernails dirtied, broken. Her knees knocked against the corners, but she didn't cry out.

She made it.

Peered through the vent.

And there he was.

A man walked into the kitchen upstairs. Big shoulders. Pressed khakis. Jean jacket. He whistled as he set two grocery bags down on the island. Tuna, soup cans, crackers, maybe a six-pack of beer. And cracked his neck like he'd just gotten back from work.

She knew she should stay quiet. But something in her. Some last flare of hope or rage or just plain human noise. Screamed loose from her chest.

"SOMEBODY HELP ME! I'M DOWN HERE!"

The man stopped whistling.

He turned toward the vent. Smiled, slow and twisted. Then he laughed.

Not a normal laugh. Not a startled laugh. A deep, throaty, amused chuckle, like he was impressed.

"Well now," he said, voice thick with mockery. "Not bad, little girl."

He walked off screen.

Then came the scraping.

Scrape.

Scrape.

THUNK.

The bookshelf slammed into place in front of the vent. The light vanished. Silence fell like a closing door.

Prince blinked.

Now he was standing in a house he'd never been in before but somehow knew. Quiet. Clean. Too clean.

Miley's home.

He heard the crying downstairs. A woman's high, cracking sobs. A man's voice, quieter, trying to contain something uncontainable.

Prince didn't look down.

He climbed the stairs, one slow foot at a time.

Miley's door was open.

He stepped inside.

It was the kind of room that made you want to apologize for being there. Not because it was messy. But because it was perfect. Lived in. Full of life that had stopped too suddenly.

The bed was made, corners sharp. Trophies lined the dresser. Math leagues, science fairs. Ribbons were pinned to a corkboard beside her desk, each one earned, not bought.

College applications lay in a neat stack. Essays printed in double space, with handwritten notes in the margins. Corrections in purple pen. Prince picked one up and read the top line:

I want to be a nuclear engineer, because energy is the future, and I want to build something that matters.

His throat went dry.

"Who are you?"

A little girl's voice. Right behind him.

Prince turned.

And shot upright. Fast, violent, breath torn from his throat like he'd been drowning. Shirt soaked. Chest heaving. The motel room was dark. Too dark. Not dream-dark. *Real* dark. The kind that didn't hide. The kind that waited.

The shadows settled around him, heavy and familiar.

He blinked. Then it was back to the slideshow.

Evans waltzing into his own ruin. That turret ripping the air in half. Bullets popping glass, chewing metal. Two men simply *gone* in less than a minute.

His fingers twitched against the bedsheet like they wanted to find the grip of a rifle.

But there was no rifle. Just a cheap room and the smell of sweat and motel plastic.

Prince exhaled. Long, trembling, ragged.

Then again.

Then he broke.

The crying came all at once. Not loud. Not childlike. But low and ugly, the kind of weeping that leaks out like blood from a split lip. He bent forward, elbows on knees, face in his hands, and shook.

He was alive. He *knew* that.

But he wasn't sure that was enough anymore.

PART FOUR

BAKER

CHAPTER EIGHTEEN

HAPPY HUNTING

DECEMBER 13, 2022

Dead men tell no tales.

Or so Prince had been taught.

The ambush at Baker's Garage had left Evans in pieces, Morris Baker's heroin-riddled corpse cold on the floor, a frenzy of news vans swarming the scene like moths to a bug zapper, and Prince with more questions than answers. The evidence was damning: photographs of young women, Miley McDermott's hoodie, Evelyn Armstrongs beanie.

It painted a picture.

Because it was supposed to.

It had been seventy-two hours since the firefight, and Prince was in the conference room at the Sheriff's Department, surrounded by crime scene photos from the garage, when Deputy Nichols knocked on the open door.

"Sorry to interrupt, Agent Prince. This just came in for you."

Nichols held out a TYVEK envelope, the type teachers used for graded assignments. No postage. No return address. Just *Agent Prince* written in neat block letters across the front.

Prince's jaw tightened. "When did this arrive?"

"About an hour ago. Found it in the mail slot. Eleanor thought it was a standard delivery at first."

Prince took the envelope carefully, examining it without opening it. "Get me a pair of gloves. And call Wilbur."

Wilbur arrived as Prince was snapping on blue latex gloves. Sheriff Haller stood in the corner, arms folded across his chest, a deep frown etched into his face.

"This was delivered directly to the station?" Wilbur asked.

"According to Nichols, found in the mail slot," Prince replied. "No witnesses. No cameras."

Prince carefully opened the envelope, using a letter opener to slit the top. Inside was a single folded sheet of paper, crisp and white. He used the tweezers to extract it, unfolding it gently before laying it flat on the conference table.

The three men leaned in to read:

Dear Agent Prince,

What's taking so long? The town's getting restless. I thought you might like an update. You should know I'm thinking of killing again. Maybe I already have. Maybe I'm just waiting.

Did I ever tell you what really happened to the Armstrong girl? She screamed in the car, so I put a tire iron through her temple. Not enough to kill. Just enough to quiet her down.

Dragged her back to my basement. It's quiet there. Clean. Just me and the tools. She woke up twice. Once from the salts. Once because I needed her to. She tried to scream again. I wrapped a belt around her throat and held her still while I took what I wanted. She cried for her father the whole time. Said something about a baby, too. That part almost made me laugh. I kept her for two days. She stopped making sense near the end. Just a hoarse little hum, like a dying bird. Then I opened her neck with a bread knife. Nothing fancy. Left her in the woods with the snow coming in. Figured the animals would get to her before the Pig Parade. But this is more fun. I think I'll go younger next time. The older ones always fight too long.

Happy hunting.

Prince felt his stomach turn. The silence in the room was deafening, broken only by Haller's ragged breathing.

"Jesus Christ," Haller whispered.

"The envelope," Prince said, focusing on procedure to keep his mind clear. "It's a TYVEK envelope." He looked up at Wilbur, whose expression mirrored his own thoughts.

"Baker," Wilbur said.

Prince nodded. "Bring him in. Now."

Three hours later, Baker sat in the interrogation room with the same expression he'd worn when Prince first met him. Slightly bored, vaguely amused, meticulously composed.

"Do you know why you're here, Mr. Baker?" Prince asked, arms folded across his chest.

"I assume it has something to do with the fiasco at my father's garage," Baker replied evenly. "A tragic situation. I understand he's dead."

"We found evidence linking your father to the murders of Evelyn Armstrong and Miley McDermott," Prince said, watching for a crack.

Nothing. Not a flinch. Just a slow, measured nod.

"My father was... disturbed," Baker said, voice lowering. "I severed most ties with him years ago. Just visited occasionally to make sure he hadn't drunk himself to death." He adjusted his glasses. The lenses caught the light like a flicker of static. "I'm sorry for what he did. Truly."

Prince didn't blink. "We received a letter today. Describing, in detail, what happened to Evelyn Armstrong."

He slid the copy across the table. Baker scanned it. His color shifted, almost imperceptibly. When he looked up, his eyes looked... off. Not glassy. Not shaken.

"This is... horrific."

Not indifferent.

"The letter came in a TYVEK envelope. Type used in school admin offices."

Baker raised his brows. "You think I wrote this?"

Calculating.

"Did you?"

"No." The answer came fast, clipped. "Absolutely not."

"Would you be willing to provide a handwriting sample?"

Baker leaned back. "Of course. I have nothing to hide, Agent Prince."

Prince slid over a blank sheet and pen. "Copy it. Word for word."

Baker picked up the pen. Left-handed. And began to write. Neat. Controlled.

Mechanical.

When he finished, he slid the page back with an eerie calm.

"There you are," he said. "I hope that helps."

Prince compared it to the original. Even without forensics, it was clear. They didn't match.

"Thank you for your cooperation, Mr. Baker," Prince said, swallowing the nausea rising in his throat. "We'll be in touch."

Baker stood, adjusting his coat like the whole thing had been a mild inconvenience. But at the door, he paused.

"Agent Prince?"

Prince looked up. "Yes?"

Baker's tone dropped an octave. No longer soft. No longer polite.

"Find who wrote that letter," he said. "Find them before they hurt someone else."

The room smelled like mildew, bleach, and old sweat trapped in the carpet. You could hear the highway whisper through the thin walls, trucks howling past like ghosts that knew better than to stop here.

Candy sat on the edge of the bed, knees together, back too straight. Like she still believed posture could keep the bad things away. Jean shorts. Plastic fur jacket. Wig blonde enough to reflect the buzz light overhead. Her nose kept twitching. Blow, probably. Or nerves.

Richard stood by the dresser. He hadn't moved since she walked in. Black T-shirt stretched over coiled muscle, dark hair slicked back like he was still trying to look clean for something. The pistol sat on the table between them. Casual, like a family photo at a wake.

"You Army?" she asked. Her voice was raspy, a throat

that had seen more smoke than air. "You got that thing. That posture."

Richard scoffed at the insult.

"Navy," he muttered.

"SEAL?"

He didn't answer.

He pulled a photo from his back pocket. Creased, grainy. A man with his arm around a teenage girl with wild hair and a drunk-in-the-sun smile. Evelyn. Frozen in time. Back when she still had a future.

"His name's Manny Alvarez. They call him Gold. You know him?"

Candy's breath caught. She did a poor job hiding it.

"Manny..." she said slowly. "Yeah. Yeah, I know Manny. Got a spot near Yonkers. Pushes coke cut with drywall and diet pills. Keeps girls around, real young ones. None of 'em stay long. Most vanish."

Richard said nothing. Just watched her. The way a hawk watches the wind.

"He's scary," she added. "Bad energy."

"Scarier than me?"

She laughed. Not because it was funny. Because she couldn't not.

"You? You ain't scary, honey. You're terrifying."

Silence settled between them like dust. Heavy. Honest.

"You gonna want to fuck, or what?"

He looked at her for a long moment. Something flickered—pity, maybe, or memory.

"Get the fuck out of here."

She signed, stood, then froze.

"You took my coke."

He didn't deny it.

"Get clean."

He tossed a hundred onto the bed like it might burn through the comforter.

Candy stared at it, then at him. Scoffed. "Really, dude?"

Richard wasn't even listening, already checking his pistol: ejecting the magazine, counting the rounds, making sure it was ready.

"You're a fucking trip, man."

She grabbed the money, then cat-whistled as she opened the door to leave.

"Go get 'em, tiger."

He didn't react.

"SEAL," she said, half out the door.

He looked up. "What?"

She tapped her nose.

"It's the way you breathe. My daddy was one. Quiet type. Had that same dead calm... usually right before he did something he shouldn't have."

The door clicked shut.

Richard stood watching the crack in the wall like it might swallow the room whole.

The handwriting analyst set down her magnifying glass. Helen Rodgers worked out of the county lab in Valhalla, a brick building that smelled of toner and coffee.

"Two different hands."

Prince blinked.

"You're certain."

"Yes."

He folded the sample, let it hang at his side.

Then he walked out.

Wilbur caught up on the sidewalk.

"So Baker's clear."

No answer.

"James."

"Yeah. Clear."

Prince pressed the folded paper through his jacket pocket. Kept walking.

"Get his records."

"Whose?"

"Baker's. School, medical. Everything."

Wilbur frowned. "Why? If he's—"

Prince broke into a run, juking snow and sleet.

"James! The car's right here!"

"I'm going for a run!"

"Where?!"

"The lodge! Get those records!"

Prince ran like a man chasing something only he could see. Wilbur had seen it before: that tunnel vision that made James brilliant and dangerous, how he folded into a case until nothing remained but the hunt, and how it always ended—doors kicked open and the truth dragged into the light, or wreckage no one could piece together.

Wilbur pulled out his phone. He'd get the records. He'd wait, because that's what partners did. The snow crunched under his boots, and somewhere in the distance James Prince was still running.

In the place where instinct lived, Wilbur knew his partner was chasing the truth. Whatever it cost. Whatever it broke.

Wilbur believed in James the way other men believed in God. Desperate, faithful, terrified of being wrong.

Twenty miles to the lodge. In this weather. James would make it. He always did.

The question was what he'd bring back.

CHAPTER NINETEEN

MOCKINGBIRD, PART I

DECEMBER 13, 2022

The silence inside the house was deafening, an unnatural quiet that sharpened the edges of Richard's senses until they were raw nerves exposed to the air.

The click of the front door behind him sounded distant, foreign, like a coffin lid settling over his body. Snow dripped from his boots, pooling on hardwood that no longer felt familiar. Not this house. Not even the hollow shape of himself stumbling through the dark.

He smelled of cheap motel soap, cocaine sweat, and whiskey—a chemical bouquet of desperation and grief. The hour spent interrogating Candy had left him dirty inside and out, caked in something that wouldn't wash off in a hundred showers.

He was tired.

Not the tired that begged sleep, but the sick exhaustion of a man who had carried death with him so long it had seeped into his bones and made nest.

He tossed his keys carelessly; they rattled somewhere far off in the dark. Didn't matter. Nothing did.

And when he walked into his office, the last thing he probably wanted to see was Janet sat there in his chair like a judge, legs crossed and shoulders square, which, for the briefest instant, infuriated him—her violation of his sanctuary. But then again, *what* sanctuary? Even this place was tainted now, every corner haunted by Evelyn's ghost, every shadow whispering accusations he couldn't silence.

Two filled prescription bottles of Zyprexa glowed on the desk beside her.

"You forget something?" Her voice was thin and sharp, barely masking anger.

He stared at the pills as if they belonged to someone else. "What?" he muttered, distant.

"Your pills," she snapped, tapping the plastic. "The ones that keep you from turning into a goddamn animal."

His jaw locked. The coke turned her words into knives. "Don't start."

"Start?" She stood abruptly. "You disappear, come back stinking of whiskey and sweat. You drinking with the whores now, Richie, or just fucking them?"

He said nothing. Couldn't. Something deep inside shifted.

"Oh, that got you, didn't it?" she sneered, eyes glittering. "Who is she? Is she younger? Prettier? Or just another gutter rat—"

He brushed past her. She struck the desk, sending the pill bottle skittering.

"Tell me, Richard. Why is Evelyn rotting in the dirt

while you, the big bad Navy SEAL, the fearless protector—her *father*—were passed out drunk when she needed you?"

He froze.

"You don't talk about that," he whispered, voice taut as wire.

"Or what?" she hissed, stepping close. "You already killed our daughter. You want to kill me too? Huh, big man?!"

His hand closed on her throat with terrifying speed, slamming her into the wall, plaster cracking behind her. Frames fell, glass shattering. Her gasp cut short as his fingers tightened, lifting her slightly, feet scraping for purchase.

"You think this is what I wanted?" Richard snarled, eyes black and burning with madness. *"You think this is the fucking life I chose?!"*

She clawed weakly at his hand, panic dawning in her eyes as his grip refused to cease. She was no longer his wife—just a target, a body, a threat. His ears rang with fury, pulse pounding like artillery fire. Her lips shaped his name, but no sound came.

Then she went slack. A sickly wheeze escaped her lips, eyes rolling backward as consciousness fled. And only then, in the silence, in the terrifying quiet of her fading breath, did he realize what he was doing.

He let go. She collapsed to the floor, coughing and retching, clutching her bruised throat as vomit spilled onto the hardwood, tears streaking her face.

He stood dumbly above her, the coke draining from his veins, leaving him hollow and terrified. Her sobs reverberated around him.

"I'm... I'm sorry," he mumbled, voice cracking pathetically. "Janet, I—"

"Fuck you!" she shrieked with wet eyes, broken and shrill, as if trying to expel every ounce of love she'd ever felt. "Fuck you, Richard! Fuck you, fuck you, *fuck you!*"

He stepped back, his hands shaking, lips trembling. His eyes—those eyes, once so sharp—looked dull, lost. Like a milky-eyed old dog who didn't understand what he'd done.

A light turned on in a neighbor's upstairs window.

Janet staggered to her feet, grabbing at walls, choking on tears, gathering herself as best she could. She limped up the stairs to their bedroom.

A bag flew down the stairs.

Then boots.

Then the scraping of keys.

He didn't stop her.

The slam echoed long after she was gone.

Richard remained motionless, the room spinning around him. The silence dragged.

Boom. He swept the remaining pill bottle off the desk. It shattered against the wall, pills bouncing like hailstones.

Then he moved. Mechanical. Calm in a way that would've terrified anyone watching.

He packed a tactical duffel. Loaded the SIG. Checked the magazine. Stowed a switchblade. Gloves. Flashlight. Zip ties. Duct-tape. Bottle of Smirnoff. His last cigarette.

His hands trembled too hard to light it, so he flung the lighter across the room. Then scraped it back up. Lit the cigarette. Stared at his faint reflection in the study window until he couldn't anymore.

By the time the sun rose, Richard's mind was gone. He was no longer a grieving father, a husband, or even a man—just something that needed to be unleashed.

Or put down.

CHAPTER TWENTY

MOCKINGBIRD, PART II

Richard sat behind the wheel of his idling truck, heat blasting, fog curling along the inside of the windshield. The dashboard glowed red. His knuckles were white around the steering wheel. A half-drained fifth of Smirnoff rested in his lap, his chest reeking of stomach acid from the bile he'd just hurled into his jacket.

He'd been awake all night. Coke residue crusted his nostrils, mouth dry and metallic. A clip rattled in his shaking hand as he slammed it into the grip of his SIG Sauer P226, checking it like a man who'd already decided to die but wanted to take the devil with him.

Across the street, a woman in a gray hoodie walked her Yorkie past the duplex. She glanced at him. Smiled, maybe. Richard didn't wave. Didn't blink. Just stared through the windshield like he was deciding if she was real. She picked up her pace.

He popped his door and stepped into the snow.

No turning back.

He crossed the icy pavement, boots crunching. Dopehouse ahead—half-rotted porch, door spray-painted black, busted light swinging above. Bass throbbed through the drywall, a broken wind chime ticking.

He knocked once. Waited.

A skinny guy with bloodshot eyes and no shirt cracked the door. "The fuck do you want?"

"Need a bump," he slurred, hunched, left shoulder angled toward the base of the door.

The man scoffed. "Man, get the fuck off my—"

BOOM.

Richard hit the door shoulder-first, splintering it off the hinges. The guy flew back and hit the floor with a yelp. Richard didn't look down. He turned right—

Three men on the couch. Blunts in hand, PlayStation controllers in their laps. They froze. One reached for the Glock on the coffee table. Richard drew his SIG.

Hellfire. One head snapped back, lifeless. The other convulsed, throat erupting in crimson spray. The third lunged sideways, grabbed a bottle of Hennessy, and hurled it.

Glass detonated against Richard's jaw, vision blurring. He staggered. Fired. Missed. The man scraped up the Glock, firing two shots that punched into drywall, raining plaster dust.

Richard surged forward, barreling into him over the coffee table, knocking the Glock free. They crashed onto stained carpet, grappling, but Richard pinned him, knee driving into his sternum.

The kid's fingers scrabbled for a pocket knife beneath

a pizza box. Richard saw the flash, snatched it first, and drove it beneath the ribs, angling upward. The man jerked once, stiffened, a strangled noise escaping him as life drained away.

Glass crunched behind him.

A shadow surged—a stocky Black man, swinging a Louisville Slugger. Richard ducked, wood splintering against plaster. He caught the man's wrist mid-swing and twisted until bones snapped. Seizing the bat, Richard swung once, striking the man's head. Skull split with a wet *snap*.

Silence.

A door creaked.

A woman—stringy hair, pupils like black holes—stumbled out of the kitchen barefoot. Kitchen knife in hand, trembling. She screamed, a sound from prehistoric times, and ran at him like a banshee.

Richard spun, catching her wrist and stopping the knife only inches from his throat. He wrenched her arm upward until the joint gave with a sharp crack, the blade clattering to the floor as she cried out.

She couldn't have weighed more than ninety pounds. He lifted her and hurled her into the wall. The sound was meat and bone splitting at once, drywall caving as her body folded unnaturally, a smear of blood marking the slide down until she collapsed in a crooked heap that no longer bore resemblance to anything human.

Behind him, coughing. The doorman—still alive. His face was a wreck, blood leaking from his nostrils as he dragged himself along the floor, leaving a trail.

Richard walked over. The man whimpered, curling into himself.

"He's in the back," he cried. "Manny's in the bathroom,

man! Back hall!"

Richard stopped above him.

The kid threw a hand over his ruined face. "Please—please—"

Richard raised the SIG.

BANG. The whimpering stopped, casing spinning on the floor.

Then he heard it—footsteps, panicked, scrambling in the back.

"Manny," he growled.

He walked through smoke and dust, boots tracking blood. At the end of the hallway, a tiny window sat open. A pair of legs thrashed, desperate to worm their way out.

"No," Richard whispered.

He grabbed both legs and yanked Manny Alvarez back inside. The man screamed, tried to twist, but Richard mounted his back, pinned him, and pulled his gun.

"No—please, bro—" Manny wheezed. "I don't even know who the fuck you are—"

Richard jammed his knee deeper into his back.

"Evelyn Armstrong."

"What?" Manny coughed, blood bubbling. "Man, Evelyn? I met that bitch, like, once. At some fucking day party last spring—"

BANG. The floor exploded beside Manny's face. A splinter tore into his cheek. He howled, writhing. Richard yanked his head back by the hair.

"Try again."

"Hey, hey, hey, I can tell you shit, I can tell you shit!" Manny cried, eyes wide and frantic. "Just don't kill me—please, ow—"

"Talk."

"It was Frankie," he stammered. "You know Frankie,

right? I saw him recently. Yeah, he came to me all pissed and shit. Said she fucked him up. Said he didn't trust her. That he wanted her gone. Asked if I knew anyone who could do it."

"And?"

"Man, I told him no! I don't do that shit. I push speed, maybe turn a few girls here and there, and I chill. That's *it.*"

"You're lying."

"I'm not!" he screamed. "I swear to fucking God, I barely knew the girl. Frankie was obsessed. He said she ruined something. Wouldn't say what. Nigga was acting all fuckin' weird. Tweaking and shit. I told fool to get the fuck out."

Richard stared—this trembling, bleeding kid with a torn cheek and piss soaking into his jeans. No malice in his eyes. Just confusion. And desperation.

"I don't even know you, bro," Manny blubbered. "I don't even know what this is."

Richard's grip on the SIG loosened. The barrel dipped, the gun hanging slack at his side as he began to pace. Manny lay trembling, cheek to the floor, one eye swollen shut, the other darting. His breath hitched.

"I didn't even know her, dog," he whimpered. "I didn't even know her."

For a second—just *one* second—it looked like Richard might walk away.

He closed his eyes. Took a breath. The kind you take before stepping off a cliff.

Then he raised the gun again.

And gave the silence another ghost to carry.

PART FIVE

THE BUTCHER OF WESTCHESTER

CHAPTER TWENTY-ONE

STATE OF EMERGENCY

DECEMBER 14, 2022

Prince sat in his motel room, staring at the evidence board he'd constructed on the wall. Photos of Evelyn Armstrong and Joyce Beckford. Maps of Bronxville with key locations marked. Timelines. Suspects.

Outside, the snow fell heavier, whirling in gusts against his window, building up on the sill. The temperature in the room seemed to drop with each passing hour, the ancient heater struggling against the encroaching cold.

Prince's service weapon lay on the bedside table, a mildly comforting presence in a town that felt increasingly hostile. He poured himself a drink, his third or fourth of the afternoon, watching the amber liquid catch the light.

His phone rang. Wilbur.

"Yeah?" Prince answered.

"Roads are closing in an hour," Wilbur said. "They've already shut down the Thruway north of White Plains. We're stuck here until this blows over."

A knock at the door. Sharp.

"Let me call you back," Prince said.

"Everything alright?"

"Yeah." Prince hung up, set down his glass, and moved to the door. He checked through the peephole.

Richard. Snow melting on his shoulders. Flushed.

Great.

Prince opened the door. "Mr. Armstrong?"

"Special Agent Prince," Richard said, his voice low and steady. "A moment?"

Prince hesitated as if he had a choice in the matter, then stepped aside, letting Richard enter.

"Let me ask you something," Richard asked without preamble, turning to face Prince. "What the *fuck* are you doing here?"

"I'm working a case, Mr. Armstrong," Prince shot back. "What the fuck are *you* doing?"

Richard laughed. "Case? You had that Lopez scum in custody, and you let him *walk*. You've been chasing shadows."

"Richard, I understand—"

"*No*, you don't," Richard cut him off. "You can't possibly understand."

Prince studied him: the tremor in his hands, the red-rimmed eyes, the tension in his jaw. A man at the edge. Prince knew when to abandon reason for performative neutrality. The lion of a man reeked of booze, iron, gunpowder, maybe coke—a nostril-betraying stench cacophony of mayhem so assailing, so horrid, it wasn't just worthy of arrest, it's oppressiveness earned claiming of metaphysical status as its own respective traveling war crime.

Richard began pacing the room. Prince, calculating—*cuffs in the left jacket pocket, six feet and one wrong word away.*

"What makes you so sure Lopez is guilty?" Prince asked, tone level.

"He's the only one who makes sense."

"There's no evidence connecting him to the crime. To any of them."

Richard didn't answer that.

Something hot and ugly rose in Prince's sternum. The hubris, the fucking *God complex.* Neutrality went out the window, the opposite sliding into place.

"You think I don't want to fucking find this monster? Huh? You think I sit here watching Oprah, playing with my dick?"

Richard stopped prowling. Locked gazes with his specialist counterpart.

"Actually, I figured the reporter took care of that." A smirk. "Cute—not like your promoted mistress in Greenwich, though. But, hey—all shapes, sizes, and shades, right? I bet your ex-wife's still insecure about that one."

Prince's temples snapped into a fast, hot thrum. Before his mind had time to correspond with his hands to form fists, Richard split into the opening leg of a sermon he expected Prince to dutifully play audience to.

"You know what I did, detective? Before I was a husband, before I was a father?"

"You were a SEAL."

"Sure. What I really did though, detective, was kill people," Richard said flatly. "In the service of my country, but dead is dead. The same way you supposedly snuff out the scum of the world with *uncanny expertise*, as some write, was how I did what I did. Same philosophy, different skill. And you know what I always come back to when I think about killing?"

Prince waited.

"There's a moment in combat," Richard said, his voice distant, "right before all hell breaks loose. A calm silence. The quiet before the storm. You're waiting, watching, knowing it's coming. Your heart's racing, but your mind? Never clearer." The whites of his eyes retreated within, reducing his pupils to black lagoons. "I felt that calm silence when I found out my daughter had been murdered."

Prince felt a coldness settle in his gut, less a prod than a DEFCON-1 siren throwing a rave within the hollow of his center. The sensation wasn't new, wasn't revelatory, but a culmination of low-frequency pings that had finally spiked into a single, tectonic roar. Suddenly, Richard wasn't the pathetic, checked-out totem of grief the country now knew him as, but another predator reveling in its proximity to an opposing force of nature. Prince glanced down carefully, a quick clocking of Richard's medieval-looking steel toe boots that had melted of snow over the duration of this inspiring chat and now...

Sure enough: blood, perfectly at home at the toe. Dark red. Hardly even crusted.

Things quickly, *horribly*, snapped into place in Prince's mind.

Van.

The thinly reported "gang shooting" he'd hardly glanced at on CNN this morning.

Shit.

"Richard, what did you do?"

"In Fallujah," Richard continued, as if Prince hadn't spoken, "there was a kid. Couldn't have been more than seventeen. Had an AK-47, pointed right at me. That was my first time feeling it. That calm silence, I saw things clearly. I could see he was just a scared kid. Just like me." His gaze hardened. "I shot him anyway. For a while, I couldn't decide if I wanted to hang myself or go out and do it again."

Richard stepped closer. "You wanna guess what I came up with?"

"We'll find who did this," Prince said, careful and measured. "The right way. We're closer than you—"

"There *is* no 'right' way," Richard snarled. "Only balance."

Prince saw it then: the dangerous certainty in Richard's eyes. The kind of warped conviction that came just before irreparable violence.

"Richard," Prince said, using his first name deliberately, "whatever you're thinking of doing, *don't*. This isn't overseas. This is your home. You're a civilian, and I *will* put you away."

Richard smiled, a cold, empty gesture that didn't reach his eyes.

"'Home'?" He scoffed. Moved toward the door. "Well, shit. In that case, I really ought to get to that home of mine before the roads close. Careful out there, agent. Fixing to be a mean one."

"Richard!" Prince snapped. "This is a blizzard. Stay off the roads tonight."

Richard paused at the door, looking back over his shoulder, both men knowing the blizzard had nothing to do with the order.

"Some storms you can't avoid. Just got to push through. Ain't that right, James?"

The door closed behind him with a soft click.

Prince stood motionless.

Motherfu—

His phone rang. Scared the shit out of him. He looked down—*Maybe: Janet Armstrong.*

"Prince," he answered.

"Detective Prince?" A woman's voice, trembling. "This is Janet Armstrong."

Prince snapped out of it. "Mrs. Armstrong. Is everything alright?"

"It's Richard," she said, her voice breaking. "We had a fight last night. A bad one. He's been drinking since, doing God knows what. He called me and just kept saying *'they're all dead'* over and over again. Started raving about Frankie Lopez next, saying the most *awful* things. Said someone had to do something. That he had his guns and he was gonna—" She broke off, gasping now. "That he was gonna hurt that poor boy. I *tried* to stop him, detective—I was screaming at the top of my lungs through the phone at him, but he just—"

"I just saw him," Prince said, already reaching for his coat. "Where are you, Mrs. Armstrong?"

"On my way to Boston—my sister's—"

"Don't stop."

Prince hung up, then grabbed his service weapon and sprinted out into the motel parking lot. Richard's truck was already rolling, taillights cutting through the falling snow.

"RICHARD!" Prince bellowed, his voice swallowed by the winter night.

The truck accelerated, crushing the motel's weathered welcome sign. Wooden splinters erupted like shrapnel, scattering across the parking lot. Prince sprinted, his shoes slipping on the icy asphalt, each breath a ragged cloud in the freezing air.

The Ram's engine roared, a deep, predatory sound that echoed through the empty street. Prince's legs burned. He watched the truck's red tail lights grow smaller, smaller, then vanish into the swirling snow.

He stopped. Hands on his knees. Breathing hard.

In the distance, nothing but white.

Richard was gone.

CHAPTER TWENTY-TWO

THE LONG NIGHT

DECEMBER 14, 2022

The blizzard had transformed Bronxville into an alien landscape. Snow blanketed everything, drifting against buildings, burying cars, erasing the boundaries between road and sidewalk. The wind howled through the empty streets, swirling flakes into miniature tornadoes that danced in the glow of streetlights.

Prince's sedan struggled through the accumulation, wheels spinning, sliding. The heater blasted at full capacity, barely keeping the windshield clear as wipers fought a losing battle against the relentless snow.

He'd tried Frankie Lopez's trailer first, finding it dark and empty. Roger Lopez hadn't seen his son since morning. The man had been worried, his weathered face etched with concern that deepened when Prince mentioned

Richard Armstrong.

If he finds my boy...

Prince was barreling toward McPherson's Steel Works in Tuckahoe. Maybe Frankie had sought shelter there when the storm hit. Maybe—

The car sputtered.

Coughed.

Died.

"Shit!" Prince slammed his palm against the steering wheel, turning the key again. The engine cranked weakly, then fell silent. He tried once more with the same result.

Stranded. In the middle of a blizzard. Miles from town.

Fuck didn't even begin to cover it.

Prince pulled his coat tighter, weighing his options. The visibility was near zero, the temperature dropping rapidly. Staying with the car was the textbook response, but Richard Armstrong was out there somewhere, armed and dangerous.

He reached for his phone. No signal.

Another set of headlights cut through the swirling snow, approaching slowly from behind. Prince's hand went instinctively to his holster as he stepped out of the car, the wind immediately cutting through his clothes.

The vehicle—*oh, for fuck's sake*—came to a stop beside him. The passenger window rolled down, revealing none other than William Baker's face, ghostly in the dim light.

"Agent Prince?" Baker called over the howl of the wind. "Car trouble?"

Prince nodded, squinting through the snow. "Battery's dead, I think."

"Hop in," Baker offered. "My place is just down the road. You can warm up, use my phone."

Prince hesitated, years of training screaming caution.

But the alternative was freezing to death in a blizzard.

"Appreciate it," he said, climbing into the passenger seat.

The interior of the Prius was warm, almost stifling after the bitter cold outside. Baker pulled back onto the road—or what Prince assumed was the road, given how thoroughly the snow had erased any landmarks.

"Lucky timing," Baker remarked. "I was heading home from the school. Had to finish grading before the break."

"Dedicated," Prince observed, hyper-aware of the man beside him.

Baker smiled faintly. "We all have our callings, don't we, Agent Prince?" He navigated a turn with careful precision. "I hear they found quite a scene at my father's garage.

"You could say that." Prince's hand stayed close to his weapon.

"I've been meaning to apologize," Baker said, his voice softening. "For any awkwardness regarding the handwriting sample. It must have been embarrassing for you when it didn't match."

Prince studied Baker's profile, the way his hands rested precisely at ten and two on the steering wheel, the controlled, measured way he spoke. Everything about the man was too neat, too deliberate.

Baker turned onto a narrow driveway that cut through dense woods. The cabin that emerged from the swirling snow was modest, its windows glowing warmly against the storm. Baker parked and led Prince inside, moving with practiced efficiency as he hung up his coat and adjusted the thermostat.

"Tea?" he offered.

"Sure," Prince said, taking in his surroundings. Nothing personal. No photographs. No mementos. Just bare walls and sparse furniture. The space felt hollow, like a stage set rather than a home.

Baker disappeared into the kitchen. Prince heard the sound of cupboards opening, water running. His attention was drawn to a door at the far end of the living room, slightly ajar, revealing a sliver of darkness beyond.

Moving silently across the hardwood floor, Prince approached the door. Peering through the crack, he could make out what appeared to be a garage. Something large was parked inside, covered by a tarp.

"The phone's in the kitchen if you need it," Baker said, reappearing with two mugs of tea. He handed one to Prince, who accepted it with a nod of thanks.

As Baker sipped his tea, Prince noticed something.

"You usually pour with your right?" Prince asked, gesturing to Baker's hand around the mug.

Baker smiled. "I'm ambidextrous, Agent Prince. Write with my left, do most other things with my right." He took another sip. "Blessing and a curse. Teachers used to try to 'fix' me in school. Make me choose one hand or the other."

Prince felt a cold certainty settle in his gut. The letter. Written by someone right-handed, when Baker had provided his sample with his left.

"Mind if I use your bathroom?" Prince asked.

Baker pointed down the hallway. "First door on the left."

Prince moved past him, but instead of entering the bathroom, he continued silently to the door at the end of the hall. The garage. He needed to see what was under that tarp.

The door creaked slightly as he pushed it open, revealing a small, neat garage. Tools hung on the wall in perfect order. The floor was swept clean. And in the center, covered by a large canvas tarp, was the unmistakable shape of a car.

Prince moved forward, reaching for the edge of the tarp.

"Find what you're looking for, Agent Prince?"

Baker stood in the doorway, his face calm, almost serene. In his right hand was a revolver, aimed steadily at Prince's chest.

"The Caprice," Prince said, nodding toward the covered car. "That's how you took them, isn't it? Evelyn. Joyce. Miley."

Baker's smile was thin. "You really should have just had that tea. Or stayed in Manhattan with that groupie you abandoned your family for."

Prince's hand moved slowly toward his holster.

"Uh-uh," Baker warned. "I'll put a hole through you before your hand even touches it."

"You set up your father," Prince said, buying time, assessing options. "All that evidence at his garage. The landmine. The sentry. You knew it was just a matter of time."

"Dad was a drunk and a waste," William Baker replied, matter-of-factly. "But useful in death, as it turns out. Everyone was so ready to believe the worst of him. Just as they were ready to believe the best of me."

His smile widened. "The beloved teacher. The mentor. The community pillar. Hell, they practically begged me to canonize myself."

"Why Evelyn?" Prince asked, inching his stance, eyes flicking around for an opening. Any opening.

"She was special," William said, his voice slipping into something almost reverent. "So bright. Wasted on that Lopez trash. Then I saw her at the gas station. After all that time. Little Evie, all grown up. I knew she was meant for me."

Prince took a cautious step forward. "And Joyce?"

"A message," William said simply. "Sport."

Another step. "And the letter?"

"A touch of theater," William admitted. "I do have a flair for the dramatic." He lifted the gun slightly. "That's far enough, Agent Prince."

Then came the sharp echo of footsteps behind him.

Prince turned just enough to see the second Baker emerge from the shadows. Identical. Gun in hand, already raised. A ghost copy with extra malice in his grin.

"He was getting too close, William," Thomas said. "Just like that spic reporter. She squealed pretty. Frankie did too, after I caved his ribs in with a baton. Sounded like a fuckin' accordion every time he breathed. Kid had heart, though."

He laughed, nostalgic. "You remember the first time Dad brought a whore home? The one with the wig and the sailor's mouth?"

William chuckled. "The one that puked on the carpet?"

"She said we looked like angels. Then made the mistake of passing out."

"She was the first," William said, eyes drifting toward Prince. "But not the last."

Prince calculated his odds. Bad. But not impossible.

He held steady.

"You know," William said, "I've never had a man in here before. Is it different, do you think? More... satisfying?"

"Fuck you."

William's grin faded. "Tell me, Agent Prince. What gave me away?"

"The tea," Prince said, hand edging toward his holster. "You pour with your right. But you write with your left."

William's brow furrowed. "Huh?"

Prince drew his weapon.

Thomas fired first. A white-hot bolt tore across

Prince's shoulder—he didn't flinch. Returned fire. Two clean shots. Chest. Center mass. The twin buckled and dropped, his weapon clattering across the floor.

Prince pivoted.

William was already firing.

Their guns thundered in unison, muzzle flashes strobing the room like lightning.

William's bullet slammed into Prince's stomach, a sledgehammer of heat and force that stole his breath. But Prince's shot landed next—between the eyes. William's head snapped back in a bloom of red.

Prince staggered. Vision swam. His weapon slipped from numb fingers as he pitched backward—

And crashed through the basement door.

He tumbled down the stairs. Wood, bone, pain, repeat. Each impact an explosion of agony, the world spinning in violent spirals, until—

Concrete. Stillness. Blood.

He came to in a crumpled heap, lungs gasping. His ribs screamed. Every breath was glass.

The flashlight rolled away, beam spinning madly across the basement. Prince reached for it—

And froze.

A patent leather heel lay inches from his face, tipped on its side like it had been discarded mid-run.

The beam crawled up.

Torn leather jacket. Lavender perfume—faint, but there, clinging to rot. A gun barrel half-submerged in packing peanuts. And then—

A hand. Slack. Pale.

Marisol.

Her recorder sat beside her hip, half-buried in dust and cardboard. Still blinking red.

Prince didn't scream. Didn't move.

He just stared—frozen in the dark, bleeding out beside a woman who'd vanished without a headline.

Prince's consciousness ebbed and flowed like the tide, pulling him under, then allowing brief moments of clarity. The basement was cold, the concrete floor beneath him colder still. His blood pooled dark and sticky, a widening stain on the dusty floor, as he coughed and wheezed.

In the dim light filtering through a small, dirty window, he could make out shapes around him. Boxes. Tools. And something else. Something worse.

Photos covering one wall. Girls. Dozens of them. Evelyn featured prominently in the center.

And beside the photos, a collection of trophies. Jewelry. Clothing. A bracelet he recognized from the Armstrong case file. A charm necklace identified as belonging to Miley—

A cough came from somewhere in the darkness. Prince turned his head, his vision swimming. In the far corner of the basement, barely visible in the dim light, was a figure huddled against the wall. Small. Female. Bound.

McDermott.

What remained of her.

The girl they'd searched for was barely recognizable. Her once healthy frame now skeletal, cheekbones jutting sharply beneath papery skin. Her eyes, sunken and hollow, held the vacant stare of someone who had endured the unendurable. Each shallow breath rattled in her chest: the unmistakable rasp of a collapsed lung.

She was a ghost, tethered to life by the thinnest of threads.

With a strength he didn't know he possessed, Prince dragged himself across the floor toward her, leaving a trail of blood in his wake. The bullet in his stomach was a burning coal, sending waves of molten agony through his body with each movement.

When he finally reached her, he saw the extent of what the Baker twins had done. Surgical cuts, methodical and precise, covered her arms and legs. Dried blood crusted around restraint marks that had worn to the bone. Her lips were cracked and blue, her breathing shallow and irregular.

"It's okay," he whispered, though he knew it wasn't. "Help is coming."

With trembling hands, he worked at the restraints binding her to the wall. Miley made no move to help or resist. She simply watched him with those empty eyes, as if she'd forgotten what hope felt like.

When the last restraint fell away, Prince pulled her gently into his arms, cradling her like he would his own daughter. Her body was feather-light, bones pressing against his chest through paper-thin skin.

"You're safe now," he told her, his voice growing weaker as his own lifeblood seeped onto the concrete. "I promise. You're going home."

Miley's eyes flickered with something—recognition, perhaps. Or the faintest glimmer of belief. She tried to speak, but only a dry rasp escaped her parched lips.

Prince fumbled for his phone with blood-slick fingers. No signal. But there had to be a way...

He spotted a small vent near the floor, rusted but potentially large enough for his phone to catch a signal outside. With excruciating effort, he stretched toward it, still holding Miley with one arm.

The motion sent fresh pain tearing through him. Black spots danced in his vision. He was running out of time.

With the last of his strength, he pressed the phone against the vent: BAKER CABIN. TWINS DEAD. SHOT. GIRL ALIVE. HURRY.

The screen flickered, then went dark as the battery died.

Prince slumped back against the wall, Miley still clutched protectively against him. Her breathing was growing more labored, the whistling in her chest more pronounced. His own strength was fading, consciousness slipping away like water through cupped hands.

"Stay with me," he whispered, though he wasn't sure if he was talking to Miley or himself. "Just a little longer."

Time lost all meaning. Minutes or hours might have passed as they huddled together in the darkness—two strangers united by circumstance, by suffering, by the desperate will to survive.

Somewhere above, a door crashed open. Voices shouted. Footsteps thundered.

"FBI! Clear!"

Wilbur's voice cut through Prince's haze. Then others. Flashlights swept the basement, their beams harsh after so much darkness. Prince shut his eyes against the glare, still holding Miley tight against him as if his failing body could somehow shield her from further harm.

"Jesus Christ," Wilbur breathed, rushing to his partner's side. "Get a medic down here! NOW!"

Prince forced his eyes open. Wilbur's face swam before him, etched with horror and fear.

"The twins," Prince managed, his voice barely audible. "Both dead. Upstairs."

"Don't try to talk, okay?" Wilbur said, pressing his hands against the wound in Prince's stomach. "Medic's coming."

"Her first," Prince rasped, nodding toward Miley. "Lu

ng... collapsed. Malnutrition. Blood loss."

Wilbur's gaze shifted to the girl in Prince's arms, his expression darkening as he took in her condition. "Jesus," he whispered again, this time with a reverence born of shock. "What did they do to her?"

Paramedics flooded into the basement, their voices urgent but controlled. Professional. Efficient. As they gently lifted Miley from his arms, Prince felt a profound sense of relief wash over him. They'd found her. She was alive. Whatever happened now, that much was certain.

His job was done.

As darkness claimed him once more, Prince thought of Zoe. Of her laughter. Of promises kept and broken.

If this was the end, at least it had meaning.

Outside, the blizzard began to subside, the wind dropping to a whisper, the snow falling in gentle, lazy flakes.

The storm was passing.

The snow fell in heavy sheets across Twin Lakes County Park, erasing boundaries and softening edges. At its center, two figures stood isolated in the storm's eye—a tableau of grief and vengeance. Richard Armstrong, once a decorated Navy SEAL, now a hollow-eyed father consumed by loss, stood with his service pistol trained on the kneeling figure before him.

Frankie Lopez, hands bound behind his back, face bruised and bleeding, knelt in the snow. His thin jacket offered little protection against the bitter cold. His breath came in ragged clouds.

"Please, Mr. Armstrong," Frankie begged. "I didn't hurt

her. I loved her."

Richard pressed the barrel of the gun against Frankie's forehead. "Give me one reason not to pull this trigger right now."

"Because I wanted the baby!" Frankie shouted, his voice breaking.

Richard's world stopped.

"She called me at school. Told me she was pregnant. I was happy, man. I wanted to keep it. I wanted to marry her."

Richard's hand wavered slightly. "What did you say?"

"I wanted the baby," Frankie repeated, tears streaming down his face, melting the snowflakes that landed on his cheeks. "She wanted to get rid of it. *That's* why we fought. That's why she was mad at me at the party. I know I'm someone you probably never wanted your daughter to be around, but I would never hurt her. I loved her."

Richard's hand trembled. The gun dipped slightly.

Frankie continued, words tumbling out desperately. "Hell, I know you hated me. But I would have taken care of them. Both of them. I swear. I'd have figured it out."

A strange calm seemed to settle over Richard. Snow fell softly in the stillness.

"She was pregnant?" Richard said finally, his voice barely audible.

Frankie's face smoothened out, his tears halting. "You didn't know?"

Richard didn't blink.

"Yeah," Frankie said, clearing his throat. "Almost a month."

Richard looked at Frankie, *really* looked at him, perhaps for the first time. The boy knelt in the snow, shoulders shaking with fear, face streaked with tears and blood. In that moment—that perfect, silent moment—something changed in Richard's eyes. A flicker of understanding, perhaps even forgiveness.

The gun lowered slightly.

And in that split-second of calm silence, Frankie saw a chance.

He lurched to his feet, hands still bound behind him, and lunged into the darkness of the trees.

The gunshot shattered the stillness with a resounding *crack*, so kneejerk Richard himself flinched.

Frankie collapsed face-first into the snow in an explosion of red dust, his skull splitting with the sound of a claw hammer driving through frozen bone. Richard stood motionless, the gun still extended, a thin wisp of smoke curling from the barrel. His face was blank, expressionless, as if he couldn't quite comprehend what he'd just done.

He walked slowly to where Frankie lay, rolling him over with the toe of his boot. The boy's eyes stared blankly at the falling snow, flakes already collecting on his lashes like frost on glass.

He dropped the gun and knelt beside him. Two fingers to the neck. No pulse.

Gone.

He hesitated... then reached forward and gently closed Frankie's eyes with the back of his hand.

He looked up, breath clouding in the cold. The sky sagged heavy with snow.

Somewhere in the trees, an owl called.

No FBI agent would arrive to stop him.

No one would save him from himself.

Prince was bleeding out in a basement across town, victim of the true killers—while Richard had just murdered an innocent boy, having not even meant to in the end. His last remaining tie to the extended Armstrong lineage. And perhaps, the one person on the planet that could've ever understood and forgiven the depth of just how far he'd fallen.

The storm would pass by morning. But Richard wouldn't.

He stayed on his knees in the snow, the calm silence around him more profound than anything he'd ever known.

And as it settled over the wreckage, he began to weep—loud, broken, uncontrollably. Not for forgiveness. Not for redemption.

But because there was nothing left to feel but pain.

CHAPTER TWENTY-THREE

IT'S OKAY, DADDY

JANUARY 21, 2023

He woke to the beat of the monitors.

Torso near-mummified. IV lodged in his left arm. The bullet from William Baker's pistol had torn through Prince's upper abdomen, skimming bone and shredding muscle, but had miraculously missed anything vital.

That's what the doctors called it, at least.

Miracle.

Prince called it luck. Especially considering he'd spent nearly two hours bleeding in that basement before Wilbur finally found him.

Jennifer sat beside him, her blonde hair pulled back in a messy ponytail, dark circles under her eyes. She thumbed through a magazine without really reading it, occasionally glancing up to check on him.

"You don't have to stay," Prince said, his voice rough from disuse.

She smiled, setting the magazine aside. "Try and stop me."

A soft knock on the door drew their attention. Tina stood in the doorway, Zoe partially hidden behind her. Brian Townley towered behind them, a steadying hand on Tina's shoulder.

"James," Tina gasped. "You look awful."

Prince managed a weak smile. "Feel worse."

Jennifer straightened in her chair, a flicker of tension crossing her face. Prince could feel the unspoken current between the two women—past and present, competing claims on his *fucked up* life.

"Daddy!" Zoe broke the tension, rushing to his bedside. She clocked the bandages. Hesitated. "Does it hurt bad?"

"Nah," Prince lied, ruffling her hair with his good arm. "Just a scratch. I'll be back on the basketball court in no time."

Tina approached the bed, her eyes softening as she took in his pale face, the IV, the monitors. Whatever anger or resentment she might have harbored seemed to fade in the face of how close he'd come to death.

One would fucking hope.

"The doctors say you'll make a full recovery," she said. "Though you should take it easy for a while."

"We'll see," Prince said.

"Mm-hmm." She glanced at Jennifer, who was watching their interaction with careful neutrality. "You must be Jennifer."

Jennifer stood, extending her hand. "Tina. It's nice to finally meet you."

The handshake was brief but civil. Brian stepped forward, his presence oddly reassuring.

"Glad you're okay, James," he said sincerely. "That was some crazy stuff up there in Bronxville. All over the news. You're a goddamn hero—"

"I should have seen it sooner," Prince cut in, the self-critique finally rising for air after weeks of medically-induced unconsciousness. "The twins. They... God, I was..." He trailed off, sniffled.

"James," Tina whispered, so gentle he snapped cold out of his spiral just to be sure it was her. "You need rest."

"You can't blame yourself, sweetie," Jennifer said, squeezing his hand. "Just relax. We're all here."

Zoe tugged at Prince's hand. "Daddy, when you get better, can we go to the park again? Like before?"

Prince looked at his daughter, at her innocent face, untouched by the horrors he'd witnessed, the evil he'd survived. He felt a lump form in his throat.

"Of course, babygirl," he promised. "As soon as I'm out of here."

The room fell into a strange, unexpected harmony—Jennifer and Tina practicing neutral small talk; Brian asking about the details of the case with ferocious curiosity; Zoe planted in the chair beside the bed, holding Prince's hand.

It wasn't perfect. It wasn't even normal.

But it was real. And that was enough.

Not because it made the darkness go away.

But because it reminded him there was still light.

Two weeks later, Prince walked through Central Park with

Zoe at his side. His arm was still in a sling, but he'd traded the hospital gown for his familiar gray sweatshirt and jeans. The winter air was crisp and clean, a far cry from the howling blizzard of Bronxville.

Zoe ran ahead to the playground, her scarf flying behind her. Prince watched her climb, jump, laugh with other children. The Armstrong case had officially closed. The Baker twins were posthumously charged with the murders of Evelyn Armstrong, Joyce Beckford, and Marisol Reyes, plus fifteen other young women in the state of New York. He called the McDermotts every day, keeping close vigil over Miley's rehabilitation—a quiet promise both gentle and unyielding, that she would never be left unprotected again.

And Prince? He was here, watching his daughter play in the fading afternoon light.

Zoe ran back to him, her cheeks flushed from the cold. She stopped, her smile fading as she noticed the tears welling in his eyes.

"Daddy? Are you crying?"

Prince quickly wiped his eyes. Zoe took his hand, her small fingers intertwining with his.

"It's okay, Daddy. I cry. So does Mommy."

Her simple acceptance broke something in him. He knelt down, pulling her into a hug with his good arm, holding her close, breathing in the scent of her hair.

"I love you, sweetheart," he whispered.

"I love you too, Daddy," she replied, her voice muffled against his shoulder.

Above them, the winter sun broke through the clouds, casting a golden glow over the park. For the first time in weeks, Prince felt something like peace.

Spring came early to Virginia, the grounds of Williamsburg Memory Care awash in cherry blossoms and new green. Prince signed in at the front desk and was assigned a guest pass with the room number 207.

He froze at 205—an involuntary stall, like his nervous system had voted no. His father's lucidity was unpredictable, fleeting, often flat-out disarming. Some days he recognized James. Some days he mistook him for an orderly. Some days he remembered his own storied career. Others, he couldn't recall his name at all. At seventy-eight, he looked older, frailer, the once-formidable FBI pioneer now reduced by the slow cruelty of dementia.

But today was a good day. Michael's eyes were clear, sharp, following Prince with the same focus he remembered from boyhood. He sat in a wheelchair by the window, sunlight soft on his face.

Michael lifted his hands. "Careful now, Lethal Weapon," he cracked. "All I'm packing is the bag they got me shitting in."

Prince smiled and pulled up a chair. "Dad. How you feeling?"

"Better now," Michael said, reaching for his son's hand. "Tell me about your case. The one up in New York. They got my Black ass watching Sesame Street. Can't find no news, no March Madness, nothing."

"It's over," Prince said, forcing a smile. "We got them."

Michael laughed. "Hell, I know that! The Baker twins, right? The boys hunting those girls?"

Prince froze. "You remember?"

"Tina and I talk." Michael tapped his temple. "Still up here—some of it. Ain't my fault you out here busy chasing tail or the devil's rejects." He leaned in, a crooked grin tugging at his face. "You really shot *both* them motherfuckers? You know the Bureau only pays you once, right?"

Prince huffed out a shaky laugh. Michael's hand tightened around his. His tone softened.

"You did good, son. *Real* good."

Those words, from this man who had rarely offered praise, who had driven Prince to excellence through example rather than affirmation, landed with unexpected weight.

"Thanks, Pop," Prince said, his voice thick with emotion.

"Uh-oh." Michael pulled his son into his lap. "Come here, boy. It's all right. It's all right. It's over, son, you hear me? It's over. You're home now. Let it out."

They sat in silence as Prince collected himself in his father's arms. Outside, life continued its relentless cycle: death giving way to rebirth, darkness to light, winter to spring.

In Boston, Janet Armstrong was slowly rebuilding. And on a quiet hillside overlooking the Hudson, its designation endorsed by the President of the United States, Evelyn Armstrong finally rested. Prince was awarded the Medal of Valor. He initially refused it, but quietly accepted, if only to redirect attention back to what truly mattered.

Prince thought of Zoe, of Jennifer, of Tina, of all the complicated web of relationships that made up his life. Of the darkness he'd survived in Bronxville, and the darkness he would inevitably face again.

But for now, in this moment, sitting beside his father in a pool of spring sunlight, James Prince allowed himself to believe in something simple and profound.

That even in the blackest night, dawn comes.

Not because it's welcome, but because it endures.

And it wins.

EPILOGUE

The house was silent, save for the rhythmic ticking of the grandfather clock.

Slow. Measured. Ancient.

Richard sat at the kitchen table, shoulders hunched, fingers loose around an empty glass. The bottle was near dry. The gun lay inches away, metal glinting in the overhead light. He hadn't touched it yet.

Three months since the night in the snow. Three months since Janet fled to Boston with Zeus. Three months since he'd scrubbed Frankie's blood from his hands, coating the basement sink in crimson.

The Bakers were dead, and the city wasted no time. By the moment the last FBI van cleared the county line, their cabin was already rubble. Miley McDermott was breathing, hidden away with her parents and being nursed back to something like life. Back in Manhattan, Prince juggled recovery, family, and the strange weight of newfound celebrity, already eyeing a summer return to the field. The case was closed.

Frankie Lopez? Missing. That was the official report. His father still put up flyers, still called the station every week. But in winter fading, so was hope. Soon, Roger Lopez would join the ranks of other parents stranded in the cruel space between mourning and belief.

No one suspected Richard. No one had seen his truck at Twin Lakes that night. No one had overheard their conversation, the accidental shot fired—*nothing*. In fact, when word spread that Frankie had gotten Evelyn pregnant, the town had all but decided he'd left out of guilt or shame. A coward's exit. And that was that.

Richard's breath was uneven, his chest rising and falling in deliberate, practiced inhales. The wind moaned against the house, oscillating hauntingly, threading through the eaves, slipping past the old wooden beams with a whisper that almost sounded like a voice.

A creak.

Soft. Barely there.

Richard's body went rigid.

Slowly, his eyes lifted.

She stood at the edge of the room, just beyond the light at the foot of the stairs.

Evelyn.

Her clothes from that night clung to her—torn in the lower back, damp. The wound at her throat was dark and yawning, dried blood stark against pale skin. Her hair, wet and stringy, framed a face that was neither angry nor afraid nor pleased. She didn't speak. Didn't move. She only stood there, silent, her gaze locked onto his.

Richard exhaled sharply, something between a breath and a sob. His lips twitched, trembled.

And then he laughed.

A small, breathy chuckle at first, slipping through his teeth. Then another, and another, until it broke into something uncontrollable, and finally the howling of a madman. His head snapped back as he clutched his ribs, high shrieks of a broken mind echoing through the cursed home, as if the absurdity of it all had come crashing down on him at once.

The grandfather clock ticked on.

Tick.

Tick.

Tick.

Outside, the wind rose into a wail. Evelyn's apparition didn't move. Somewhere in the back of the house, a hinge let go—brief, missable.

And so Richard laughed, and laughed, and laughed, until his vision blurred, until the sound spilling out of him felt no longer his own, until it was no sound that should ever come from man, until—

Click.

Everything stopped.

AFTERWORD

I remember first pitching *Violent Crimes* to my high school film teacher in 2018.

To preface, he didn't like me much. Double-preface, I don't blame him. I challenged everything he said about movies, not always because I disagreed, but because it was first period, I had a couple buddies in the class, and I thought arguing made me clever. Truth is, I liked him. He was funny. Smart. Had taste. About 6'5, 350 pounds, built like a Kryptonian linebacker with Letterboxd opinions.

Of course, I hadn't met the world yet. Didn't even know it existed. What a surprise that would be.

The assignment was simple: write a five-minute short. Check. I walked in the next morning and handed him what would become—emphasis on *become*—*Violent Crimes*. It was a small, technically ambitious short (Budget: One (1) potato, also known as the Canon Rebel T3i, and maybe twelve bucks if I didn't blow it on Chipotle later) set between a home office, a friend's car, and a woods clearing behind the school. It starred a grieving father and veteran named Richard Armstrong. His daughter, Evelyn or something like that, was dead. He was taking justice into his own hands. Detective Wilbur was on the case. The whole thing ended with a *punch*. Richard gets a call after the deed is done—they'd caught the real killer. BOOM. He'd taken out the wrong kid. BOOM. He crawls into bed next to his wife, hollowed out. Fade to black. I imagined a standing ovation at TRIBECA.

Mr. H. blinked. Then, flatly:

"Yeah... no."

"Why not?!"

"There's no story!" he said with a wheeze, like he was explaining to a toddler why they couldn't build a roller coaster out of couch cushions and gum wrappers. "It's just a guy shooting someone. Where's the beginning, middle, and end?"

At the time I wanted to throw him out the window. Which is funny considering I was about a buck forty on a good day and he was taller than me sitting down. Odds are I would've gone flying like a raccoon hitting a semi and class would've gone on like nothing happened.

Seven years later—after a few deaths, some ruin, and a whole lot more life than anybody could ever be ready for—that five-page script with no story became my debut novel—and defining crucible—that laid the foundation for the rest of my career. But it had to rot a little first. It had to burn off the bullshit I was hiding behind and drag me face-first into the part of myself I kept pretending wasn't there, had to break me in places I didn't even know were *there*. It had to get written wrong, then written worse, then gutted on the floor at three in the morning while I wondered if I even deserved to call myself a writer. And if I didn't? Well, let's just say we would've had a bigger problem.

I always circle back to the same question. *Why?* Why this book, this world, these shattered characters. But I'm starting to think that answer isn't for me. Maybe it never was. Maybe the only thing that matters is that I loved this story enough to survive it. Enough to let it break me open and put me back together with sharper edges. And if I had to, I'd walk through every inch of that fire again.

Because the people the world kindly calls writers—we're not in this for comfort, are we? We do it because something in us refuses to die quietly. Because there's a strange, electric *aliveness* that comes from holding the weight of a world built out of our own bruises, our own longing, our own quiet agony channeled through a keyboard in a dim-lit room at the edge of exhaustion and bankruptcy.

Violent Crimes was not the loudest thing I ever wrote, or the most expansive, or the most technically ambitious. But it was the first story that demanded I earn it. The first that cared more about honesty than polish, more about atmosphere than architecture. It turned five pages of teenage bravado into a fully breathing world—dark, wounded, moral, furious—and in doing so, it turned me into a different kind of artist. One who couldn't hide behind aesthetics or pacing tricks or detached cynicism anymore.

Like its author, *Violent Crimes* just needed to grow up a little. And in doing so, it forced me to.

The truth is: nobody makes anything worth half a damn alone. Sometimes your collaborators are friends, or your mom. Sometimes it's a throwaway moment after your first short story where your girlfriend tells you she prefers Abbycat *Group* to Abbycat Entertainment. Sometimes it's the film teacher from seven years ago telling you you're out of your fucking mind.

So Mr. Hoffman, thank you. For the easy mornings talking movies. For the laughs. For sparing my neck. For grounding me. This one's for you, wherever you are.

To the readers: this was *Violent Crimes.* If you loved it, I'm flattered. If you hated it, I probably deserve it.

Godspeed.

ACKNOWLEDGEMENTS

Thank you to my mother, for none of this would be possible without you. Your grace, kindness, strength, intelligence, and empathy are the foundation of everything I do. Everything I accomplish is for you. I love you. To Mulan: thank you for always being by my side. To Nic Pizzolatto: you showed me there were no limits, that brutality and poetry, philosophy and pulp, could live in the same body and still matter. You helped me find my voice before I even knew it had a place. To Aunt Linda, for always showing up, and to Uncle Steve, whose encyclopedic flat-screen television knowledge and impeccable wardrobe remain undefeated. Thank you both for everything. To my late father, Darrick Chase: still the funniest man I ever knew, still my hero, still the voice in my head keeping me from completely losing my way. I love you. And to the others who helped this book, and me, find the light: you know who you are.

ABOUT THE AUTHOR

JACK CHASE is an American novelist, short story writer, essayist, and the founder of Abbycat Group & Publishing Brands. He is known for *Made in America: or The Tragedy of Billy Castle and Unexpected Absolution of Dean Willis* and *The Bastard of Taylor's End*. He has been regarded for his storytelling range, morally complex characters, and prolific output, releasing twelve books in his first year of publishing. He lives in Southern California with his cat, Mulan.

WELCOME BACK AGENT PRINCE

Three years after the events of *Violent Crimes*, **Special Agent James Prince** travels to Los Angeles with his wife and teenage daughter for what should be a quiet spring break visit to UCLA.

But when **three aspiring actresses are discovered brutally murdered** in a Brentwood apartment—accompanied by a haunting poem signed **"The Black Butterfly"**—Prince is drawn into a labyrinth of Hollywood ambition, beauty, and decay.

Violent Crimes 2: Black Butterfly. 10.31.26. **Preorder now**.

www.ingramcontent.com/pod-product-compliance
Lightning Source LLC
Chambersburg PA
CBHW020912310726
48980CB00011B/845/J

* 9 7 9 8 9 9 8 6 3 8 8 8 6 *